A Way Yonder

Dick Blizzard

authorHOUSE®

AuthorHouse™
1663 Liberty Drive
Bloomington, IN 47403
www.authorhouse.com
Phone: 1-800-839-8640

Published by AuthorHouse   10/04/2014

ISBN: 978-1-4969-4485-6 (sc)
ISBN: 978-1-4969-4484-9 (e)

Chapter 1

The Navigator

For six exhausting days and restless nights we pitched and rolled in the grip of a relentless gale. HMS Cumberland was moaning; her decks were creaking. Storm sails billowed forward, twisting and straining the tall wooden masts. Our decks were awash with frothy seawater. Below decks huge timbers were grinding and growling in defiance to the rolling waves. Sailors were flung and tossed as they scampered about high in the rigging. We were locked in the awesome power of nature. Our course held true by a competent crew.

It is different now. The ocean is calm and the crew is relaxed. A half moon reflects back from across the smooth sea. Cumberland is steady as she goes. She is swaying easily in a gentle swell. It is strangely quiet, except for a faint ripple created by the ship's bow slicing through the still water. Captain Merritt has ordered all storm damaged sails down for repairs. Small stabilizing sails are rigged on the foremast; they hang limp, except for an occasional flutter.

The Florida Peninsula beckons to us from across the vast Atlantic Ocean. Mandy and I are working to pay our passage to America. We are assigned to the officer's mess; we help the cook feed the captain and his officers.

A junior officer has taken a shine to my 15 year old sister. Lt. Jack Games is short. He is just a bit taller than Mandy. He is a muscular, well groomed and a clean shaven young man. Jack is a gentleman. He has spent the previous two years cruising the Pacific and Indian Oceans. Lt. Games has chosen the life of a seafaring man.

Except for Jack, Mandy and I have been mostly ignored.

Then, without warning, the navigator looks directly at me.

"Charles McKenna!" He yells across the room. "How old are you?"

"Eighteen." I am startled, but I answer the bow-legged navigator quickly. I take the opportunity to ask, "Sir is this ship moving? It seems we have stopped. Are we in the doldrums?"

"Yes, we are moving. The wind has laid a bit, but we are being carried toward the Americas by the sea current. The doldrums are some distance south of here - near the equator." The navigator wobbles toward his favorite chair.

The cook sees the navigator coming and jumps up. He motions for Mr. Bloom to take his seat.

"But, how do you know we are moving?" I ask as politely as possible.

"I check our position with the sextant every day." Mr. Bloom, our navigator, is 2nd in command, behind the captain..

"Sextant?" I can't believe he is actually talking to me.

"Yes, a sextant. It is an instrument that measures the angle from the ship to the sun and stars. After I get the angle, I go to my books and plot our position on the Captain's chart."

"Is that it?"

"Well, I must know the date and get the exact time from the ship's chronometer."

I give him my puzzled look.

"It's just a fancy clock, son"

I'm not completely sure what he is talking about, so I just nod.

"Tell me", he barks. "Why did you and your sister leave your home in Ireland and set out for America?"

"Mandy and me, we were kicked out of Ireland, because Mandy got convicted of murder." That commanded everyone's attention, especially Mandy's suitor.

"Got convicted? Sounds like you don't think she did it." The navigator's voice is a little more polite this time.

"She sure as hell didn't do it. I killed that fat bastard myself," I said proudly.

Mr. Games and all the officers laughed - I laughed, too. The navigator smiled.

"You killed him! Well now, tell us all about that. It's a long voyage. We have plenty of time to talk."

"Where should I begin?" I was nervous.

"Why did you kill him? Was it self defense?"

"No. He raped my little sister. I just snuck up behind him and sank a double bladed ax into his skull."

"You hit him from behind. Didn't you think he deserved a fighting chance?" The navigator has an insincere frown frozen on his round face.

"I didn't care about that. I just wanted him dead."

"So, you were defending Mandy." The navigator sounds like he's okay with that.

"Yes. I did it to keep her safe. He was going to kill her, for sure."

"How old was she?"

"Eleven. She was just eleven years old. It happened almost four years ago."

"Where was your father?"

"Daddy was dead already. He got killed by a bull almost a month before."

"Killed by a bull? How did that happen?" The navigator settles back into his chair and waits.

Everyone is looking at me and waiting for me to speak. So I start...

It was a cold day and we were following the funeral cart up to the hill top cemetery. The path was steep and it was rough; barely wide enough for the cart.

"Your dad's body was on a horse cart?" The navigator pulls his chair up closer.

"Yes, it was a one-horse cart."

It only had two wheels, but they were big wheels. The horse was big, too. That big buckskin mare didn't have any trouble getting Dad up the rocky path to the hilltop cemetery.

We had two helpers. They had already dug the grave. Mandy and me - we didn't have any money, so I guess the preacher paid them with church money.

The navigator nodded, so I kept talking. Mandy was wearing our dear departed mother's winter coat. Her little hand felt cold to me, but I think she must have shut out the pain, because she was smiling that day.

"Did your Dad have a coffin?"

"Yes, it was a wood coffin. The church got it for us."

"You're lucky you didn't have to bury him in a shroud." The navigator takes a sip of rum.

"The village mortician knew we didn't have any money, so he refused to tend to our father's dead body. Mandy and me, we had to get him ready for the grave. She carried hot water from the fireplace to the bunk where they had laid him. Dad had a hole in his gut were the bull gored him. He stunk pretty bad. Mandy tried to clean away the dried blood and crud from his body. Her tears kept falling down on Dad's chalky skin. She just used the tears to help clean him. She kept crying harder and harder and she was rubbing faster and faster. After a while, I reached over and took the rag from her hand. I told her to quit rubbing on him. Then, we dragged the coffin over close to the bunk. I grabbed Dad under his armpits and Mandy got his feet. We lifted him up on him a little and then just slid him into the box. I was trying to hold up, but when we picked him up, I just broke down; he felt so cold and stiff."

"We were both crying, but we got him into the coffin all right. I quickly nailed the lid shut. He was naked, so I nailed fast."

"You buried your father naked?" The navigator was wearing that frown again.

"Yes, he was cold and naked, but I was warm".

"I was warm for the first time that winter because I had taken all the clothes from dad's dead body and I was wearing them. Mandy wanted to cover him up with an old quilt from her bed, but I told her that Dad was already in a warmer place. She put the blanket on him anyway."

"I was getting tired of walking up cemetery hill, so I grabbed on to the horse cart for a pull. I was tugging my sister along behind me. Mandy had picked a fresh daffodil and she was carrying it in the crook of her arm. I'll never forget how pretty she was. She had her wine colored stocking hat pulled over her ears and down low onto her forehead. There was just a little of her curly red hair sticking out from under her hat. She had freckles all around her nose. Daddy liked to tease her about her freckles."

"Girls sometimes have bad feelings for a Dad who drinks." The navigator speaks like he is asking a question.

"Mandy liked Dad even though he was a bad drunk. I think she liked him because she knew he loved her. Yeah, she liked him a lot."

"Keep going." The navigator gives a yawning wave with the back of his hand.

"We helped the gravediggers get the coffin off the cart and into the grave. After we got Dad down into the ground, those two gravediggers stood back with their heads bowed. They were trying to show proper respect, but I could tell they just wanted to fill the hole and be off to the pub."

"I have a worn-out pocketknife. I took it from Daddy's pants pocket. The bone handle has loosened and it wiggles a little. The blade has been sharpened so many times it is thin and razor sharp."

The navigator reaches for my knife. "Is this all you got?" He doesn't look up and voice is low.

"Pretty much all I got."

"Mandy has a broach craved out of ivory. She got it when Mom died. There were some bottles of whiskey hidden under the floorboards at home. We had a little cow waiting in O'Malley's pasture. The cow was carrying a calf. That was all we had."

"Where did you live?"

"Dad rented a one-room house for us after Mom died. It was a good warm house, but most everything inside belonged to the landlord."

"Were you satisfied with the funeral?"

"Dad got a proper funeral but it was not in the church".

"Pastor O'Rourke was dressed in his black suit and his white collar. He was shaking from the cold, but he had some good things to say about Dad and Mandy and me. The Reverend had never seen Dad in church, so he probably just wanted to say, He was a good man, Lord, but he was bad to drink - cover him with dirt boys, and let's get out of the cold. Instead, he prayed the Lord's Prayer, and then he said something about dust-to-dust, and added some happy words about a reunion in heaven.

I remember he said this too. "He was a good man, Lord. Please have mercy on his soul, Lord. And Lord, please accept him into your heavenly fold. And merciful Lord, please protect and provide for these poor children he left behind." He said Lord a lot, but Mandy didn't hear it, because she was watching some chipmunks playing under a big tree just outside the cemetery. I figured she was pretty much stupefied by her grief."

"When the Reverend got through preaching, he put his Bible away. That must have awoken Mandy. She stepped to the edge of the grave and tossed in her daffodil. She stooped down around her feet and picked up a double handful of the freshly dug dirt. She tossed the dirt in on top of the coffin and then she went over to the horse cart and picked off a smooth stone she had selected from the rubble down by our house. Mandy placed the stone on the cairn in the middle of the cemetery. That stone is a marker for Dad. The only marker he will ever get, I guess."

"Were there many people at the cemetery?" The navigator asks.

"No one came. I was surprised when no one came."

"What about the church people?"

"We didn't go to the church? Dad didn't like going to church."

"Are you religious?"

"Some. We both believe in God, and Mandy has learned her bible pretty good."

9

Tom O'Malley played Amazing Grace down in the village and we could hear it really good up at the graveyard. Mandy and I love Tom's music and Dad liked that song.

"That's the sweet sound of O'Malley's bagpipe," I whispered to Mandy. She smiled.

"When we came back down the hill into the sunshine, the day was brighter. It was warmer, too. I could hear the dirt and rocks being shoveled onto the wood coffin. I was relieved it was finally done, but it was a sad time."

"I could tell Mandy was alright because she was talking about springtime. The trees were starting to bud and there was a sweet aroma floating on the breeze. The neighbors had built a fire in our house and I saw smoke coming from our chimney. I could see people carrying food into the house."

"Tell me more about your dad." The Navigator is pumping me.

"Well, when he was sober, Dad was a good hard working man, but he was a mean drunk. He was drunk a lot."

"Was he a big man?" The navigator wants details.

"Yes. He was big and powerful strong. Whenever we went out, if Dad saw another big man he sometimes wanted to wrestle him, just to see who was the strongest."

"You mean, who was the stronger." The navigator corrects.

"Yes, that's right and Dad won most every time."

I remember one time though, when a big Hunky man pinned Dad down pretty fast. Those Hunky's are all Gypsies, you know." The navigator nods, but he looks a little puzzled.

"Would you say your dad was a handsome man?"

"Women thought he was good looking, I guess."

"He had some girlfriends after Mom died. He brought some of them to our house to get them into bed. Some of them girls yelled and moaned a little, but they all thought he drunk too much."

"How did he manage to get himself killed?"

"Well, I'll tell you"…

Earlier that week, I was over at the O'Malley place. Shelly and me were playing up in the hayloft. She was my girlfriend. We overheard Tom talking to Dad.

"You mean, Shelly and I."

"Yes, we were hiding in the barn loft."

I heard Tom say really loud, "I'm sorry Will! You just can't take Rufus out of the barn yard, but you are welcome to bring your heifer over here and leave her with him."

"Why can't I take him and walk him over to our place, Tom? Rufus has that ring in his nose - I can just lead your big bull along like a puppy dog." Dad said.

"If that horny critter got a whiff of a possum in heat, he'd drag you half way across the county- ring or no ring. He won first prize at the fair the last three years in a row for his aggressive nature." That made Shelly giggle.

"But what if he don't do nothin' when I put my heifer in there with him?" Dad knew better. He just wanted to take Rufus out and show him off.

"If your little heifer is in-season, he'll do something for sure." Shelly laughed so loud I had to put my hand over her mouth.

"Well, all right then, I'll bring the heifer over here tomorrow." Dad sounded disappointed.

"I won't be home tomorrow. We are going to market. Just get her in the pen fast or Rufus will try to burst out to her. I don't want to find his blue-ribbon balls hanging on that barbed wire fence when I come back home. After your heifer is in the barnyard and the gate is locked, you just open his stall and get out of the way. He won't need any help." Tom warned.

That made Shelly laugh. She buried her face in the blanket and laughed so loud, I thought they would hear her.

"Why did you care?" I think the navigator knew the answer to that.

"Because Shelly and me were snuggling up there in the barn loft. I was afraid if her Uncle Tom found us, he would raise all manner of hell."

"Was Shelly pretty with her clothes off?" That question brought me a vision of Shelly's snow white breast and beautiful flat stomach, but I just pretended I didn't hear him.

"Don't you know that society doesn't approve of playing in the hay with a woman if you're not married?"

"Well, we are married now, so I guess it was all right. Anyway we couldn't help it. It just happened."

"Why isn't Shelly on this ship with you?"

"She wanted to wait until after the baby is born. Then she's coming to America on the very next ship."

"Why wait?"

"There ain't nothin but smelly men with dirty hands on this boat. Who would deliver the baby?"

"There's an old Negro woman down in the bilge of the boat. I'm sure she's delivered lots of babies."

"Negro? I have never seen a Negro woman. I've never even seen any black person."

"Well, you don't want to see this one either. She's crazy. She kills chickens down there in the bilge. She drinks chicken blood and spreads blood all around, and she prays to her Voodoo Gods."

"What's the bilge?"

"The bilge is the very bottom of the ship."

"And we have chickens down there?"

"Sure do. That's where our fresh eggs come from. We also have some goats for milk and cheese."

"I thought I smelled goats."

"You didn't smell any goats. That's why they are way down in the bilge. Bertha can shovel the manure out the port hole and it doesn't stink up the boat. The wind blows the smell away from us."

"Bertha? Is that the Negro lady's name?"

"Yes, but she's no lady. Get on with your story." The navigator grins.

"The next morning I went with Dad and our little heifer walked right into the big bull's barnyard. That heifer knew the horny bull was in there and she was ready for him. Dad ran into the barn to release the bull. Rufus weighs over a ton and he had already been drove crazy by the scent of our heifer.

I heard the big bull burst out of his stall and I saw Dad grab the rope dangling from Rufus's thick neck. When Rufus felt Dad pulling on the rope he just lurched forward. Dad was whip-slung into the barnyard and up against a stone wall. He was gored in the stomach when Rufus rammed him up against the rock. The bull's left horn went all the way through Dad's gut and that's what killed him. I climbed up on the side of barn stall and I saw that Dad was hurt bad. He was bleeding and slumping down the wall."

"How old were you when all this happened?"

"Fifteen", I answered quickly and continued.

"Rufus ran right over and started fuckin the heifer with Dad's blood and slimy guts still hanging on his horns. The heifer was so little I thought he was going to kill her too, but she was all right. They were making some noises I had never heard before. Rufus was snorting and the heifer was making a moaning sound and grunting.

I was hanging on to the side of the barn stall and starting to feel a little weak. I sure as hell didn't to fall into that barnyard with Rufus all riled up."

"Son, you should say 'breeding', instead of that 'F' word." The navigator likes to teach.

"Why?" I ask.

"Well, breeding is a more genteel word and it is just like fucking". He assures.

"It might be more genteel, but there ain't nothing just like fuckin'!" I came back with a good one.

All the officers laugh until we hear Mandy yell from her bunk. "Shut up and go to bed!"

The navigator motions for Mr. Games to close Mandy's door.

"Dad's eyes were open and he was smiling, but he was dead all right. Mandy thought his eyes were open because he saw the angels coming for him.

"The angels made him happy, so he smiled," she said.

"Do you believe that angels come for you when you die?" The navigator is lighting his pipe and he is getting hard to hear.

"Maybe?" I had never thought about angels.

"Keep going,"

"The night after we buried him I was at home in front of a hot fire. I was sipping Dad's homemade liquor and trying to remember the good times. Mandy was asleep. She was sunk deep down in her feather bed. I could see by the light from the fire that she was resting well. The fire had small yellow and orange flames licking from the hot coals. White-hot sparks kept popping out; they were hypnotizing me. Sparks were flying fast up the chimney and shooting out into the cold, clear night."

"Sounds like you were doing well." The navigator observes.

"We were fine that night, but the landlord arrived early the next morning. He came on his horse to talk about the rent. He is the man I killed."

"You killed him because he came to collect his rent?" The navigator says with a grin.

"I already told you, he raped and beat Mandy. It wasn't about the rent. I knew he was due his rent." I am trying not to get irritated with the navigator.

"Tell me more about the landlord" The navigator is smiling, so I guess I didn't offend him.

"Well, he came in the house and he started talking."

"Charles McKenna you have some tough times ahead, for sure." The landlord said.

" He was talking to me, but he was watching Mandy. She was stirring the fire to make a fresh pot of tea. Mandy hung a teapot on the iron hook over the fire."

"Yes sir, I guess so." I was mumbling and I tried not to look directly at that smelly man who Dad always called "that fat bastard".

"Your rent is due in fifteen days. Will you have my money?" He squeezed his words out between coughs and wheezes.

"I will have the money for sure!" I was thinking I could sell off some of the whiskey Dad left us.

Mandy approached us with our dear mother's ankle length dress dragging the uneven wooden floor. She was balancing three tin cups of steaming tea on a serving board.

"Please sir - a taste of tea before you go?" Mandy was almost singing her words.

We sipped the tea slowly. It was hot and Mandy was proud. She liked being the lady of the house. The landlord's eyes were locked on my sister. He was making me nervous.

Suddenly, the landlord stood up and walked toward the door.

"He failed to offer his condolences for our departed father, and he did not thank me for the tea, nor did he say goodbye. He definitely has a rude manner," Mandy was talking low and out the side of her mouth.

McQuirk's bony horse stumbled to one side when he swung his stubby leg across and settled into the saddle.

"I'll be back in a fortnight to collect me rent," he yelled without looking back.

"Tell me some more about that O'Malley fellow." The navigator hands me a tin cup with a swallow of rum covering the bottom.

"Tom O'Malley is a rich man. He's big, too. Tom's not very tall, but he has a big chest and his shoulders are wide. His shoulders are uncommon wide. He always wears big sheepskin suspenders. The suspenders keep his pants pulled up high in his crotch and his belt buckle is almost up on his chest. Tom O'Malley is as strong. Strong as an ox."

"You say, he has a big farm?" I can tell the navigator wants to hear all about Tom.

"Yes, a big farm."

The farm is in the rolling hills not far from our little one room shack. Tom and his family graze a big sheep herd. Their niece lives with them. That's Shelly, the girl

I married. Shelly is still there, and Aunt Sally is taking care of her, because Shelly is pregnant. Tom and Aunt Sally have four grown up children. They are all married and have families of their own. All the children live in the village, but they work on the farm. They work hard and they live well.

"What about the house? Does your wife have her own room?"

"Yes, she has a nice room with a good bed."

"Shelly's room is downstairs and Tom and Aunt Sally are upstairs".

"Tom's ancestors built the main part of the house. The main part is two stories high. Those ancestors just gathered the rocks they found in the fields and built the house. Years later, Tom's grandfather built on two wings; one on each end of the house. He built the wings out of wood. After that, a kitchen room was added in the back by Tom's dad when Tom was little. Tom told me all about this. The house has three big stone chimneys and the roof shingles are imported cedar. It's a fine house."

"Does he have lots of other animals besides the sheep?" The navigator is starting to doze off, but he wakes up every time I quit talking. So, I keep talking.

"They have four big draught horses in the main barn. That barn has cows and milking stalls on one end and the big horses are on the other end. There are always five or six donkeys picking grass out in the pasture. When it gets dark or a storm comes up the donkeys go under a 'lean to' on the side of the barn."

"What about Rufus?"

"Tom keeps his prized bull in a special barn. Rufus grazes in his very own pasture. He is kept behind a stonewall fence. Tom has three strands of barbed wire on top of the rock fence. Rufus just stays in there until his services are needed. He breeds a lot of the cows in the village."

The navigator is pleased with Tom's selection of words.

"There are lots of dogs. There is always a bunch of those black and white sheep herding dogs running around the place. Seven or eight of the dogs are always well trained and working. They are smart dogs and they are easy to train. Herding sheep is just born into them dogs and Tom likes to train the young ones."

"Does Shelly help herd the sheep?" The questions keep coming.

"Shelly feeds the chickens, ducks, geese, cats, rat dogs and the big hunting dogs. They all just run around free and it is hard to walk near the house without stepping in something. Shelly helps Aunt Sally cook and clean in the house. She works hard every day. Shelly likes to work."

"Shelly's mom and dad were both drowned. Her dad was a ferryboat captain. He owned the boat and they ran it back and forth from Ireland to England. Shelly's mom worked on the boat, too. She took care of the passengers with tea and sandwiches. One night during a storm the boat caught fire. The boat sank and everyone died. Shelly was just four when all that happened."

"My God, I remember that. They found the burned out hull washed up in the rocks on the South Coast of England. Almost thirty souls were lost at sea that night." The navigator sits up straight and leans toward me. He blows a little pipe smoke toward me and his voice is serious.

"I can sense you don't you like O'Malley. Why? He seems like a good, hard working man."

"Well, for one thing, he wouldn't give me my cow back after Dad died. She was carrying Rufus's calf."

"Tell me about it." The navigator yawns.

I went to get our cow and when I saw him I said, "We are obliged to you, Tom O'Malley, for pipin' that nice hymn to honor our departed father, Mandy and me, we are truly grateful."

"It was nothin' Lad. Will McKenna was an old friend," O'Malley was full of crap; he didn't even like my dad.

"Where's my heifer?" I asked outright.

"Tom looked at me and he didn't say anything for a while."

"That animal belongs to me now," O'Malley finally said.

"What?" I yelled back at him.

"Your dad owed me money; more money than the worth of that little cow. I will keep the heifer, and we can call the debt paid - paid in full." He said.

I couldn't believe what he was saying.

"I have the notes, lad -- and I have talked to the magistrate. Sorry Charles, but I'll be a keepin' her.

Then, with a smile, O'Malley pointed to a nervous nanny goat with a rope around her neck.

Tom was trading us that goat for our cow, I figured."

"Her milk is richer than cow's milk and she'll eat anything - no need for a pasture and she never needs to go to water, she gets all the water she needs from the weeds and briars she eats."

I turned to look at the goat.

"Mandy can make you some good cheese with her rich milk. Take her, she's free!" Tom was gesturing with his big rough hands.

I just grabbed the rope and started walking. I headed for home, knowing I have been cheated. My only friend lied to me and he stole my property. I planned to sell that pregnant cow for good money."

"You'll be a needin' to hang a bell around the goat's neck. She likes to wander about looking for something to eat." Tom was yelling after me. The little goat was pulling and bucking as we stumbled around the hillside path."

* *

Chapter 2

Rape

"So, you had a goat, some whiskey, a pocketknife, an ivory broach and the clothes on your back." The navigator is counting with his fingers. "You had a girlfriend, but you didn't have a job. How did you plan to survive?"

I was trying to figure that out when Reverend O'Rourke called Mandy and me to the church. I knocked on the door of the pastor's study. "I'll be right out." He shouted through the closed door.

The Methodist Church was cool and quiet when Mandy and I got there. Mandy was sitting on the front pew with her hands on her knees, looking at the stained glass window behind the pulpit. She liked being inside the Church, I could tell that.

After a while, Reverend O'Rourke came out of his study and into the sanctuary. His footsteps were echoing back from the empty choir loft. It was really loud, but you could tell by the way he walked that he had a lot of respect for the church.

"Young lady," the Pastor said, "The Church is concerned about your welfare and we have found you a home with a family that has agreed to feed, clothe and shelter you."

"A family?" Mandy was surprised.

"Yes. The McQuirk's will take you in and they will care for you."

"That landlord man?" Mandy mumbled with a frown.

"Yes! You must agree to this arrangement or the county will draft an order to have you committed to the orphanage. The McQuirk's will provide a good home for you."

"I'll just stay with my brother. He's all grown up now and we'll get along just fine."

"Mandy, you have become the responsibility of the county. If you don't go live with the McQuirks, it is off to the orphanage for you."

"Mrs. McQuirk is a nice lady, but I can't abide by her fat husband," Mandy tried to swallow her words, but it was too late.

"Now that kind of disrespect for your elders is not acceptable in God's House. I'll come for you in the morning. Go home now and get your things together."

Later that day, Mandy told me she had finally decided to go live with the McQuirks, I was surprised!

"You can't stay with the McQuirks. The old lady is addled, and what about that lunatic boy that does nothin but tend to his pack of dogs." I yelled.

"Millie McQuirk is very nice and that crazy son of hers hasn't been seen since last year." Mandy said. She is poking at the fire and not looking at me.

"Well, I don't like the way that old bastard looks at you, and some people think he killed that boy and threw him down the old well. You and me - we need to be together, so I can protect you!"

"I'll just try it for a while. It might be all right. I don't want to go to the orphanage."

The navigator has fallen asleep in his chair. His head is on his chest and he looks uncomfortable. I just leave him there and go into our bunk room. Mandy is already asleep.

I was half asleep myself when I recalled this conversation with my sister four years ago:

"Why are you late? Have you had anything to eat?"

"Shelly and I went for a swim in the river - Shelly fixed a picnic." I said.

"She is so pretty. She told me she liked you. Did you kiss her? Are you going to get married?" Mandy teased.

"Married? Don't you think I should get a job first?"

"Do you love her?" Mandy has always been direct.

"I don't know. Maybe I do love her."

"Have you made love to her?"

I just ignored that question.

"She has beautiful auburn hair and she has a very nice figure." Mandy says.

"She is young, and I am not going to do anything to make her not like me."

"Maybe she wants to make love. You should ask her very politely the next time you are alone together."

"No. I don't think so. She might be scared or embarrassed. She might slap my face or something."

"It is probably better to wait until she tells you she is ready. She will tell you without saying anything."

"How would I know if she doesn't say anything?"

"You'll know."

"You're only eleven. How do you know so much about love?"

"Girls know." Mandy said with a little smirk. I asleep well.

Next morning, Captain Merritt is at his place at the head of the table. He is going over his ocean charts and waiting for his coffee. Mandy and I are out of our bunks early. I get the fire going in the cook stove and put on a big pot of coffee. Mandy places the bowls on the table. We feed six officers and the captain three meals a day. Captain Merritt always has big bowl of oat mush for breakfast, and he has a private stash of apples and limes in his cabin. He keeps his fruit in his cabin and it is Mandy's job to make sure he doesn't run out. The navigator and the other officers prefer eggs and cheese and pork jerky. We warm up some hard biscuits for them to dip in their coffee...

As usual, the young British officer is flirting with Mandy. He pats her on her bottom as she is pouring his coffee. In return, Mandy pretends to pour hot coffee in his lap.

The navigator says, "Mr. Games you should use caution. Mandy is wanted for murder."

"I didn't kill him, but I wanted too." Mandy adds quickly and gives Mr. Games a dirty look.

"We must hear about this." The navigator pleads.

"When?" Mandy surprises everyone.

"Now!" The officers say in unison.

"She's not going to tell you anything," I yell.

"It's alright Charles. I'll tell the story."

Mandy begins...

I pled guilty to the charge of murder because they were going to hang my brother. Millie McQuirk knew they wouldn't hang me, so Millie swore on the Holy Bible that she saw me kill her husband with an ax. She said she was praying for Jesus to forgive her for telling a lie the entire time she was testifying.

After Dad died, I had the choice of going to the county orphanage or I could go live with the McQuirks. I wanted to stay with Charles, but they wouldn't let me. So, I agreed to go live with the McQuirks.

"Was McQuirk also your landlord?" The navigator wants details.

"Yes. I didn't like him at all, but his wife was nice."

I had seen Millie in town a many times. She came to church on Christmas and Easter.

We had to walk for over a mile though the forest to get to their house. The house was up a steep hollow and it looked spooky. There was a creek that ran right under the porch. The creek was nasty. A dead dog was being held under a rock by the current just downstream of the house.

Millie was waiting for us on the porch steps.. I could tell she was expecting company, because she was wearing a stiff white crocheted collar under her black dress. Millie was thin and bony and she looked older than her husband. I asked her were her boy was, and that pack of dogs of his.

"My boy ran off last year and there ain't nary a dog on this place." Millie declared.

The preacher told me to keep quiet.

"Mrs. McQuirk you and your generous husband will go to heaven for sure for taking this orphaned girl into your home." It sounded like the pastor had rehearsed that.

"Thank you, Reverend." Millie looked toward the heavens and placed her hand over her heart.

"Where is your husband?"

"He went to the mill to have some corn ground." Millie was lying; she crossed herself.

"Well, I must return to the village. I hope to see you in church next Sunday; bring your husband." Pastor O'Roark heads down the rocky path. I watch him until he is out of sight. I feel scared, and I am alone.

Millie took me up to my room. It was up in the attic, but it looked okay. She showed me the outside steps and told me to use them if I had to go out to the toilet late at night or anything.

That night after supper, I helped Millie wash the dishes. It was already dark, because McQuirk got home late and he showed up pretty drunk. Millie and McQuirk were sitting by the fire. He was wheezing and coughing and Millie was knitting. I started to sit down and Mr. McQuirk told me to go on to my room.

It wasn't long 'till I heard him coming up the stairway. He didn't knock and as soon as he came into my room he tried to rip off my gown. I spat at him and I scratched his arm. Then he hit me with his fist and I fell down. He started kicking me in the head.

That's all I remember until I woke up in the infirmary three days later. Shelly was by my bed and she told me that McQuirk was dead and that my brother, Charles, was on death row in the county prison.

Mandy has never talked about the rape before and she is trying hard not to cry.

"How did you find out she was hurt?" It was Mr. Games and it was a moment before I realized he was talking to me. I had never heard Mandy tell that story before and my mind was kind of numb.

I answered his question…

"After she left home, I was all alone."

The first three nights, I didn't sleep much. I spent the nights watching the shadows from the fire play across the ceiling. I learned to milk the goat and traded some of her milk for some eggs and cheese. I managed to sell two bottles of the whiskey that Dad left.

I wanted a regular job and I missed my little sister. I decided to go see Pastor O'Rourke and demand that Mandy be brought back home.

"I can't bring her back home until she reaches legal age, but McQuirk might give you a job and you could live there, too." The Preacher wrote me a letter of recommendation and addressed it to the McQuirk's.

I got up before dawn the next day. With letter in hand, I started out at first light for McQuirk's place.

"Hell no! You can't see your sister and I ain't givin' you no work neither. Now get off this place and don't you ever come back here again!" McQuirk was out of control; he had a pint of grog in his left hand and he was flailing a cocked pistol around in his right hand. He dropped my letter of recommendation and stomped it.

I was not afraid of that old man, but I was really scared for Mandy. I decided to leave and think about what I should do before McQuirk got careless with that pistol.

"Come back at sunset – *I'll let you see her!*" Millie McQuirk whispered to me as I passed close to her. I was walking fast, but I heard her good.

I was shocked that Millie was brave enough to 'cross' her crazed husband. I knew for sure that the scrappy little old lady was taking quite a chance with her own life by inviting me back to see Mandy.

Why would Millie do that? Can I really trust her or is she setting a trap for me? All this is circling around in my mind. I had no choice. I had to go back.

I waited out in the woods until dusk. I crossed over the ridge to a sunken thicket and built a little campfire. I had a hunk of goat cheese and a pint of whiskey. I sat close to the fire and ate the cheese and drank Dad's whiskey. I began to plan my strategy.

I had a snoot full of whiskey by the time darkness started to fall. I decided to climb up to the top of the ridge and circle in behind the house and then come down the steep hill to McQuirk's back door; just in case they were planning an ambush. I couldn't be completely sure the old woman hadn't set me up for a bushwhacking, but I had to take a chance, if I was ever going to see my sister again.

A huge yellow moon was rising through the trees on the far ridge. The moonlight was behind me and I could see Millie standing on her front porch with her back to me. She was searching down the hill trying to get a glimpse of me coming up the path in the moonlight. I was glad there were no dogs guarding the house. That hill behind the house was steep and I mostly slid down the slope on my heels. I had to grab onto the trees and bushes to stop myself.

The barn was above the house. McQuirk's skinny horse was locked inside his barn stall. The horse knew I was out there. He could smell me, and he could hear me flailing about in the darkness. The little gelding started to neigh and whinny, and he was stamping and kicking about inside his stall. The skittish horse created quite a racket and it caused the old man to squirm and grunt some. I could see McQuirk through the open door. He moved around a little in his big chair. He felt down by his side for his pistol, but he didn't stand up.

I stopped, and I was frozen in place until the horse settled down. After a bit, the gelding was quiet. I whistled softly down the hill toward Mrs. McQuirk. She turned quickly and she looked toward me in the moonlight. I stood up tall and waved both arms. She made a quick motion for me to come in out of the dark woods.

"Here's the key to her latch. Take the steps on the outside of the house to the upstairs room," she whispered. "Mr. McQuirk is dozing by the fire – hurry now!"

The steps were narrow and there was no handrail. I crawled up the steep steps on all fours. The boards were squeaking and I was cursing them under my breath. I reached the landing outside Mandy's room and knocked lightly on her door. I called her name.

There was no light coming from the little crack under the door and there was no sound coming back to me from the darkness. I fumbled with the key until the rusty lock snapped over. The warped door popped open and a whiff of stinky air rushed out. The room was cold and dark.

As my eyes began to adjust, I could see the dim glow of a small candle.

I felt my way across the room. I was hunkered down and stumbling across the uneven floor boards toward the flickering of the candle. I picked up the little candle and used it to find my sister. She was on the floor over in the corner. Her body was curled into a tiny ball.

When the candle lit up Mandy's face, her eyes were swollen shut and her face was bruised and puffy. She was covered with dried blood. I couldn't even tell it was Mandy until she uttered a grateful little moan. She was clutching a broken table leg for protection and her dress was torn away from her little breast. She had a dirty woolen blanket under her battered head.

"Did he rape you?"

Mandy couldn't speak, but she shook her head, "yes".

"I'm going to kill that son-of-a-bitch!" I heard someone yelling; it was me.

I gently removed the table leg from her swollen hands and crawled through the darkness toward the door. I went bounding down the steps. I was making a lot of noise.

The old lady was standing at the bottom of the stairs. She was holding a big double bladed ax in her bony hands.

I thought, "Well, I'm going to have to kill her too!" She just smiled and handed me the ax.

She offered a little advice. "Sneak up behind him and whack him good. He is full of grog, but he still has that pistol."

And "whack him good" I did. When I finally came to my senses, the ax was stuck deeply down between his shoulders and his greasy head was laid open like a ripe melon. I was vaguely aware of a death gurgle bubbling from McQuirk's severed throat.

I could hear the old woman giggling merrily behind me. She was dancing about and she was shouting, "Praise be to God".

Relief flooded my mind and body. I was relaxed and I was thinking, "That old woman is a little touched!"

Then I became aware of warm goo covering my body. Blood was gushing from the old man's neck and I was being showered with a sticky red bath.

"Hurry along home now and wash up!" the old lady warned. She handed me a towel. "I'll take good care of your little sister. She will be safe here now."

I ran toward home in the darkness. The trees were thick and there was an arbor of branches hanging over the wagon road. The moon was bright and it created shadows and patterns along the road.

There were a lot of critter sounds coming from the dark woods. I could hear howling, barking and grunting. I could hear the grunts of the wild pigs. I saw galloping, orange eyeballs reflecting through the brush. The flashing eyeballs were keeping pace beside me. I was running fast. I was running for my life. I was covered with McQuirk's blood. I was terrified.

Fear fueled my body. I seemed to possess great strength and agility. I lengthen my stride and ran like a deer fleeing a wolf pack. The moon helped me see well enough to avoid the pitfalls in the road. I knew if I stumbled wild pigs would be on top of me in an instant!

I was sure that God was sending the pigs to kill me and eat me, because I had committed willful murder. I started to scream out into the darkness. "Please someone help me! The sharp sound of my voice echoing through the darkness made me feel safer. I knew there was no help out there, but the yelling gave me comfort and it refueled my efforts.

Soon, I ran out of the woods and onto the moon lit ridge. The dim lights of my little village began to appear in the valley below…

I awoke flush with terror. The nauseating stench from my old prison cell has permeated my nostrils and I could hear footsteps coming for me. Slowly, I become aware that I am no longer on death row - no longer awaiting the gallows. I am safe aboard the HMS Cumberland on the way to a new life in a new world.

I'm awake, but the dream continues…

The jailer and the hangman came to my cell to check my weight. "If you ain't heavy enough, the noose won't break your neck when you fall, so we will hang some iron from your ankles to make you heavier. If your neck breaks quick, you won't feel no pain." The hangman is in my face and he is wearing a ghoulish smile.

It was then that I realized they were really going to kill me!

The jailer came again the very next day. I was paralyzed with fear. He sensed my panic and he laughed the entire time he was getting me ready. "Wash up. Here are some clean clothes. The judge wants to see you. I'm sure you are going to get good news. The judge never calls prisoners to his chambers for bad news." The jailer is a compassionate man.

"Charles McKenna, I have revoked your death sentence. You are free to go!" The judge was peering over his glasses waiting for my reaction.

I was frozen to my chair and could not speak. The judge nodded to the jailer and he came right over and unlocked my leg irons. He picked up the irons and clanked noisily out of the room without looking back. I could not believe he was leaving me there unguarded and unchained in the judge's chambers.

"What happened, Judge?" I was dumbfounded.

"Millie McQuirk was here this morning and she told me she witnessed your little sister kill Mr. McQuirk with an ax." The judge paused and stared at me again. I knew he wanted me to say something.

"Millie saw Mandy kill him with her own eyes?" I can only chirp. My throat is tight.

"Yes! I have been taking testimony for a lot of years, and I am sure Millie McQuirk is telling the truth. You are free to go!"

"Will they hang my sister, Judge?" I know they will not hang her, but I asked the question with the most concern I can muster.

"No, we don't hang little girls, but she will go to the asylum for three years, and then I will decide what to do with her."

The judge scooted his chair back. I stood up to leave without being excused.

"Just one minute, Charles. Tell me again how you managed to get covered with blood on the very night that Mr. McQuirk was murdered."

I sat back down and I repeated my story about being attacked by a pack of wild hogs. "That big sow I stabbed was right on top of me and she bled all over me."

I could tell the judge wasn't totally convinced, but it is irrelevant now. He motioned for me to leave with a blank look and a wave of his hand.

My girlfriend and my little sister were waiting right outside the judge's chambers. Shelly's pretty blue eyes were swollen and her beautiful nose was red and dripping. She was trying to smile, but her lips were trembling. The three of us hugged, cried and laughed, all at the same time. We held tightly to one another for a long time.

After a while, the custodian entered the room. She gently took Mandy by the arm and guided her toward the door. They stopped and turned near the door, so Mandy could say goodbye. Mandy still had bruises on her face and her broken right arm is in a splint. Her lips and her eyes were puffy. She could not speak, but she forced a little smile and she mouthed the words, "I love you". The door closed and she was gone - gone to pay my debt. I felt numb, but full of admiration and deep concern for my little sister.

Soon after I was set free, Shelly and I were married.

It was months before they finally let us visit Mandy at the asylum. We found her sitting in the middle of a big room full of sick people. Disturbed people were chattering and milling about. The room was noisy and Mandy was sitting on the floor in the middle of the room. She was wearing a dirty cotton gown. The sleeves of her gown were tied behind her back and her arms were crossed across her chest like a straight jacket. Shelly and I got Mandy under her arms and lifted her up onto her feet. We untied the sleeves. She was surprised to see us and she let out a big scream of joy.

"Shelly, you are so radiant and beautiful." Mandy touches Shelly's cheek.

"Bet you can guess why." Shelly is wearing a big smile.

"Oh Goodness, you're pregnant!" Mandy screams.

"Yes, three months now." Shelly pats her belly.

"When did you get married?"

"Three and a half months ago." Shelly is okay with telling a little lie.

"Do you want a boy or girl?"

"I want a boy and Charles wants a girl." Shelly smiles at me.

"He does?" Mandy knows better.

"We just want a healthy baby and I am praying Shelly will be just fine though it all." I am sincere.

"I'm so happy. I've got to get out of this place, so I can hold my nephew." Mandy wants a boy.

"Tell me all about the wedding." Mandy's eyes are beaming.

"Well, Charles and I went to Reverend O'Roark and asked to be married in the church, but our pastor thought I was pregnant, so he said no." Shelly's smile morphs into a frown.

"Pregnant. How could that be?" Is Mandy serious?

"Well, we decided to get married down by the river." Shelly didn't answer Mandy's silly question.

"That spot where you used to picnic?"

"Yes, the very same spot." Shelly gives me a sexy smile.

"What did you wear?"

"I wore my old cotton dress. It was the dress I used to swim in. Charles loves that dress."

"Why did you like that dress so much, Charles?" Mandy is waiting for an answer.

"Well, she didn't ever wear anything under it when we went swimming. When it got wet, I could see her beautiful body right through it. I could see her flat tummy and cute butt and that tiny patch right below her belly button. The cold water made her pink nipples push though..." I have gone too far.

"Stop it. I get it." Mandy is blushing.

"What else?" Mandy looks directly at Shelly; she's heard enough from her brother.

"I was barefoot and I had a red rose in my hair."

"We didn't know the preacher, but he married us for no charge. I made him an apple pie."

A gigantic shout of joy came out of Mandy's mouth. It caught the attention of the attendant. A big muscular woman with coarse gray hair piled up in a big bun on top of her head came over and re-tied Mandy's sleeves.

"We keep all our violent inmates and the criminally insane secured. It is for their own safety as well as the safety of others – this girl is a convicted murderer." The big woman gave us a look of warning, before she left to attend to a ruckus on the other side of the room.

Mandy has been locked up for almost three years now, so Shelly and I went to the judge to plead for her release.

The judge spoke sternly, "I did not say I would release her after three years. I said I would evaluate her. Here is a report I just received from the asylum; it is not good. Mandy is disobedient and uncooperative and deemed not ready to return to society. The warden thinks she needs more time; more time to mature and learn to control her emotions."

But, the judge did make us an offer: "I will release Mandy if she agrees to leave Ireland immediately. You must arrange for her passage out of the country. Come back to see me when you have made the arrangements."

Several weeks passed before I could arrange for passage to America. Mandy and I agreed to become 'indentured servants' and work on board a ship to pay our fare. We agreed to work during the voyage and then for two more years after arriving in Virginia. Shelly will stay with Aunt Sally until after our baby is born. I should be able to pay for her and the baby by that time.

We took our papers to the judge and he promised to release Mandy just two days before the ship sets sail and he kept his promise.

Captain Merritt waited for the tidal current and the wind to favor Cumberland's departure. He must use the elements to his advantage if he is to depart the crowded harbor without incident.

Favorable conditions for our departure occurred at sunset. The crew rigged two small sails – a jib forward and a steering sail aft.

The setting sun was a flaming orange ball. The evening sky was aglow. Shelly was standing on the wharf watching us glide silently away. She could hear the officer's yelling commands as the tidal current moved the gigantic wooden ship slowly away from the dock. Cumberland was proud and graceful as the breeze filled the mainsails. She headed purposely toward the open sea.

Shelly was smiling and waving to us from the dock. Mandy and I were standing on the rear deck waving furiously. We hope to see Shelly again very soon.

"Where is the big ship going?" A stranger on the dock asked Shelly as the sails faded into the misty glow.

Shelly points toward the sun's sinking halo and spoke softly with a tear on her cheek.

"*A Way Yonder*." She whispered.

Chapter 3

The Captain's Daughter

Mandy cautiously follows Mr. Games through the hatch and down the ladder into the lower decks of the ship.

"We are going down into the cargo hold. There are no light ports down here." He speaks softly as he lights a whale oil lamp.

"My goodness, I didn't know all this stuff was down here, Mr. Games." The cargo hold is full of bags of seed and grain, hardware in wooden crates, and tools.

Mandy is breathless. This is the first time she has ever been alone with Mr. Games. They have developed a mutual attraction during the first three weeks of the voyage, but they have never been alone, until now.

"Call me Jack. Please call me Jack." He says as he slowly moves closer.

"Yes, Jack." She closes her eyes and waits for his kiss in the faint flicker of the lamp.

Mandy is almost sixteen and her first real kiss has caused an intoxicating glow to surge through her body. Her mind is spinning and she feels faint. She eases herself down onto the bags of grain, with Jack's lingering kiss softly following her willing lips.

Jack blows out the lamp and he finds Mandy anxiously waiting in the pitch-black darkness.

He asks her if it is her first time.

"Yes, but don't worry, love will make it happen." Mandy is singing her words.

Jack moves slowly with purpose. Time stands still. The lovers become locked in a floating bubble of ecstasy.

Reality returns when the 'ship's bell' rings-in the hour of midnight. Jack is late for his duties on the bridge. His watch as "officer of the bridge" starts at midnight and goes until 4 am – he is late.

Jack hurriedly pulls on his uniform shirt and he gives Mandy a glancing goodbye kiss. He scurries up the ladder toward his duty station dragging his trousers.

Mr. Games will assume command of the ship a few minutes late and his tardy arrival must be entered into the ships log. The log is reviewed daily by Captain Merritt.

The next morning the cook and I are scrambling about to feed the officers their breakfast without Mandy.

"Where is Mandy? She has never missed her breakfast duties." Jack is obviously concerned.

My sister and I always serve the early meal, and we clean up afterwards.

Mr. Games looks at me and repeats his question, "Charles McKenna where the hell is your sister?"

"I don't know, Mr. Games. I thought she was with you."

"I have been on duty since midnight. I left her in the cargo hold." He looks to see if that has made me angry.

I am not angry. I approve of Mr. Games' attention to my sister, but I am not ready to tell him that.

After Jack left her, Mandy made her way down through the cargo hold hatch and into the ship's bilge. She is in the very bottom of the boat stumbling toward a flickering candle, and searching for black Bertha in the darkness.

"Bertha's over here, baby." The Voodoo Priestess lights more candles so Mandy can see. Mandy is scared. She has never, ever, seen a black person before in her life. Bertha is tall and curvaceous and her skin is a creamy golden brown. When Bertha smiles her teeth sparkle brightly in the dim light. The whites of her eyes are clear and bright. Mandy is struck by Bertha's casual beauty. She is wearing a long loose gown. The gown is orange tinted yellow and it is trimmed in black. It hangs to the floor. Bertha picks the gown up in the front when she moves.

Mandy had expected that Bertha would be a little dirty and much older, but she sparkles with youth and vigor.

"Oh my, you are a pretty girl! I am so glad you came to see Bertha. Why do you look so sad, baby?"

"I think I am dying Bertha. I am bleeding really bad, but I don't hurt."

"Show me." Bertha commands.

Mandy lifts her dress and Bertha laughs. "Where is your Momma, child?"

"Momma died when I was nine."

"And no one told you this was going to happen to you when you became a big girl."

"What has happened?" Mandy is scared.

"Open you blouse and let Bertha see you." Bertha takes a quick look and motions for her to button up. Mandy's small breasts are perky, pink and pretty, but Bertha does not comment.

"You are not sick, baby. You are just becoming a woman. You are no longer a little girl. You can have a baby now."

"Really! I thought you had to be married to have a baby."

Bertha laughs until the tears are streaming down her round cheeks. "No child, you don't have to be married to have a baby. You really haven't had any mothering, have you? Bertha will teach you some things."

"I heard you and Jack making love up there in the cargo hold last night. You may have a love child in your flat little belly real soon if you and Jack keep that up. Do you want to have a baby?"

"No! Oh God, no."

"Are you going to make love to Jack again?"

"I guess so, he is teaching me. I can't help myself. I love him, Bertha."

"You love him? You think you love him! My, my, Bertha had better make a potion for you." Bertha always refers to herself in the third person.

"Before you met Jack, did you know anything about making love? Bertha wants to know more.

"Yes." I knew a lot. After Mom died, Daddy would bring girls home from the tavern and they would make love." Mandy has a sad look on her pretty face.

"Did they do it in front of you?" Bertha sounds concerned.

"No, but we lived in a one room house and they always thought I was asleep." She's still looking sad.

"Wasn't it dark?"

"Yes, except for the fire light."

"What did you think about it?" Bertha asks the big question.

"I kind of liked it. I had already seen the animals do it. I didn't know people did it."

"Anything else?"

"They were always drunk, so I wondered for a long time if you had to be drunk."

"No, but it helps sometimes." Bertha is obviously speaking from experience.

"Jack is going to bring some rum next time." Mandy finally smiles.

"You come back after your work is finished tomorrow morning and your galley is all cleaned up. I will have a potion cooked up and ready for you to drink. The potion will keep you from having a baby. Now, you had better get back up there before they come down here looking for you."

"That dress you are wearing is dirty. Bring it back down here to me. Bring all your dirty clothes; Bertha will wash them for you." Bertha hands Mandy a damp cloth.

"You don't have to wash my clothes, Bertha. I know how to wash clothes."

"You bring them back to me. Bertha puts all her dirty clothes in a net and drags them along beside this big ship on a rope. They get nice and clean and fresh after a few hours."

"Do you put soap in the net with the clothes?" Mandy is excited about the prospect of having cleaner clothes.

"No need for soap. The salty seawater cleans and bleaches everything just fine. You run along now before they turn this ship around to see if you fell overboard."

"When will I quit bleeding Bertha?"

"You will quit in two or three days, but it is going to happen again next month. Look at the moon. When the moon looks the same next month, it will be your time."

"Next month?"

"Yes, every month from now until you are an old woman. If you don't bleed, it means you probably have a baby in your tummy."

"Goodness that's awful. Thank you, Bertha. Goodbye. I'll be back tomorrow." Mandy is relieved to know she is not going to die.

"You come back down here and see Bertha tomorrow. We will talk some more and you can drink the potion I make for you." Bertha holds the candle high so Mandy can find her way to the ladder and then up to the cargo hold.

Mr. Games and I are coming down the ladder just like Bertha predicted. We meet Mandy going up. She knows we are looking for her. Our concern is showing.

Mandy looks tired and she tells me that she is sick and is going straight to her hammock and rest. She gives Jack a quick 'see you later' smile and she climbs up the ladder toward her bunk.

Mandy is all right, but we can't help but wonder what she has been doing down here in the darkness since midnight.

Mandy keeps her little talk with Bertha a secret.

The HMS Cumberland has been moving steadily under a moderate wind and ocean current for several days now. Big waves are swelling up behind the ship and the swells are pushing her along toward the Caribbean. The weather is getting warmer each passing day. The sailors are lowering themselves on long ropes into the warm water.

There is a "buzz" going through the ship. I sense that something exciting is about to happen!

After breakfast, Mandy sneaks back down into the bilge to see Bertha.

"Bertha, why is everyone so giddy all of a sudden?."

"We are just a few days away from Mosquito Island. The Captain's woman and both his children live there. Many of the ship's crew members have women and children on the island."

"Jack, too?"

"No, not Jack, this is his first trip to America, but he probably has a woman in Africa or India." Bertha doesn't try to hide her sly smile.

"I know Captain Merritt has a wife and a family back in England. He writes letters to them in his stateroom." Mandy has secretly read a poem that Mrs. Merritt gave to her husband before he left to face the perils of the open sea.

"Yes, and the Captain has a wonderful woman and two beautiful children on Mosquito Island and we will be there with them in just a few days."

"This is very troubling to me Bertha. I am sure two wives is against the law."

"Yes, it is against the laws of Ireland and against the laws of your church, but the laws of nature are powerful. It is not unusual for seagoing men to have several families – you will soon learn the ways of ocean going men. Besides, what you and Jack are doing up there in cargo hold is not exactly approved by the church either."

"Does Mr. Bloom, the navigator, have a woman here, too?" Mandy quickly changes the subject.

"No, Mr. Bloom doesn't have a woman here. I have never seen him with a woman, or heard him talk about a family." Bertha looks at Mandy for a reaction.

"Well, I guess he will not be going ashore." Mandy surmises.

"He always goes ashore. He has men friends." Bertha can tell that Mandy knows nothing of men who like men, but she decides to let her figure this one out for herself.

"Oh, how nice!" Mandy is sincerely naive.

"Does the church approve what you and Jack are doing up there in the cargo hold?" Bertha wants an answer.

"No it doesn't, Bertha, but, Jack and I are in love! There is nothing more holy than love." Mandy is deadly serious, and working around the issue.

"Love is good, but remember, it can be complicated", Bertha says. "Follow your heart, baby! Life is short and happiness comes and goes in bunches."

Bertha searched through the boxes and bags up in the cargo hold and found the 'makings' for the morning-after potion she has mixed up for Mandy. It is a formula known only to a Voodoo Priestess. She hands the cup to Mandy and commands, "down the hatch". Mandy drinks it all down and makes an ugly face.

"Every time you make love to Jack, I'll cook you up a potion so you won't have a baby before you're ready. You are just a pretty baby yourself."

"Thank you Bertha."

Three days later, Mandy and I wake to find the ship securely anchored in a cozy little cove on the south side of Mosquito Island. Most of the crew has jumped over the starboard side of the ship and they are splashing about in the water busily washing their bodies and scrubbing their clothes in the warm, salty, emerald green, clear water of the Caribbean Sea. There is a flood of chalky white bodies going and coming near the back of the ship.

Jack tells Mandy and me that we should jump in and refresh our bodies.

"Go over on the port side of the ship, away from the naked crew. I'll join you soon." Jack commands.

In the early afternoon a small boat approaches the Cumberland with a young man rowing. An older man is the only passenger. Captain Merritt receives the native elder at the starboard side boarding ladder. The Captain is wearing his three cornered royal blue uniform hat for the first time since we left the harbor in Ireland. The hat is trimmed in gold and his jacket is a matching blue. The jacket's wide lapels are also trimmed in gold. It's a three quarter length jacket with split tails. The jacket is open in the front except where it is held together with a single large gold button.

The Captain has donned his "dress blues" to honor his old friend, Ramon.

Ramon is the Island Chief. He is outfitted in his best white short pants and he is wearing a colorful orange and green shirt. The shirt fits loosely and it blows away from the old man's body when the cool breeze comes. They proceed to the Captain's cabin and close the door behind them. The meeting begins with a cup of rum and a cigar from the Captain's private stock.

"Captain Merritt, my dear friend, how are you?" The wise Island elder is graying, but he stands straight and his eyes are beaming. Ramon is genuinely fond of Captain Merritt.

"I am remarkably fine, how is my old and cherished friend." Captain Merritt is completely at ease.

"My people are coming with lots of fresh spring water for you." Ramon is proud of his service to the big ship and to the United Kingdom.

"We have all the items you requested except they only boarded 50 vials of smallpox serum." The captain's tone is apologetic.

"Do you have all the sulfur drugs we requested? Ramon looks concerned.

"Yes. And you have two big jugs of ether. It's all in one crate."

"Thank you." Ramon leans back in his chair and takes a swig of rum followed by a draw on his cigar.

"What can you tell me about my family?" Captain Merritt asks.

"Well, your children are nearly full grown and Lila is very beautiful. Your son calls himself, Douglas, now. He is a fine young man." Ramon waits for the next question.

"And, my woman, how is she?"

"She is well and happy. She has a good man living with her now. He is the Island carpenter." Ramon expects the captain to react angrily.

There is silence; a long uneasy silence.

"Does the carpenter get along well with the children? "The captain appears unhappy, but he shows no anger.

"What is his name?" Ramon is not volunteering much.

"They call him Spencer." The Chief says politely.

"Does he know about me?" "Will I be welcome?" The captain looks Ramon in the eye.

"Yes, of course, he remembers you and you will recognize him when you meet him."

"I will?" Captain Merritt is sure it will be awkward.

"Yes." Ramon's short answer indicates that is ready to change the subject.

"Your daughter is looking for a man. You may be a grandfather soon."

There is a knock on the door.

"Enter." The captain shouts.

"Sir, Chief Ramon's boat is overloaded. He may want to make two trips or call for another boat," Mr. Games waits for an answer.

The captain looks to Ramon for his decision.

"It's a short ride in calm waters. We will do it in one trip." Ramon stands.

Outside, the crew has been busy loading the island boat with gifts and medicine and other items of need. The gifts are tagged. Most all the crewmembers put gifts and trinkets on board before it heads for shore.

Ramon carefully boards the heavily laden boat. The helmsman carefully rows toward the island, with the old man sitting regally in the bow. He is making a lot of smoke puffing on his complimentary cigar.

Soon after the Island Chief departs, six large boats arrive with wooden barrels filled with fresh drinking water from the island's spring. There is a group of young men and women in each boat. The heavy barrels are hoisted aboard with the ships crane and empty barrels from the Cumberland are loaded into the island boat. After the work is finished, they tie off their boats and climb the rope ladders for an uninvited, but welcomed visit. As always, the islanders are in a party mood. More boats arrive with more fresh water. After a while, a host of young island people is celebrating on the decks of the Cumberland. Some of them are dark skinned; many have lighter complexions – they are all attractive, happy people. Everyone is excited and freely mingling with the freshly bathed crew. There is lots of talking and laughing; old friends are hugging and kissing and dancing about.

Mandy is mystified. She is totally disgusted. She heads for the bottom of the ship to talk to Bertha.

"I don't like it Bertha. How long will we be stuck here? I want to go on to Virginia." Mandy is pouting.

"Bertha knows a secret place where we can watch the party and stay out of sight. Follow me." Bertha is whispering for effect.

The two new friends climb up the ladder to the cargo hold. It is dark, so Bertha holds Mandy's hand as they make their way aft though the bags, bales and boxes to a rickety ladder in the back of the cargo hold. Bertha goes up the ladder first and slides open a small hatch. They climb into a little space that is just big enough for the two of them. There is sunlight coming in between the cracks in the wall; they can hear the happy voices coming from the main deck of the ship and see the on deck happenings through the cracks clearly.

"Bertha can see the Captain's two beautiful children!" Bertha sounds happy. "Look how tall and pretty they are – my how they've grown." The captain's son and daughter are leaning against the rail straight across the deck from us. They are both wearing loin cloths; Douglas is shirtless and Lila's cotton shirt is still wet with the Caribbean salty sea water.

"Oh my goodness, she is so beautiful! She is talking to my brother! She is standing too close and pushing herself up against him." Why doesn't he move back? I'm going right out there right now and tell her Charles is married." Mandy is furious.

"That will make no difference to Lila. These peaceful island people have a culture of free love. She is a spoiled brat and she gets whatever she wants."

"Well then, I'll just go and explain to her that Charles and Shelly have a baby on the way."

Bertha just smiles as Mandy heads down the ladder. She makes her way across the cargo hold in the darkness. Little sister is determined to position herself between the island princess and her brother.

"Mandy. Come and meet Lila. She is Captain Merritt's daughter." I stand tall and yell and wave across the deck to my sister.

The island beauty turns and smiles at Mandy. Lila's cotton shirt is still wet and her body is pushing through the thin fabric. The shirt reveals all - it is clinging to her small waist and it perfectly outlines the soft muscles in her flat stomach and you can see an imprint of her tiny belly button. She has a skimpy bright green and loose fitting, cloth tied around her full hips. Lila never bothers with under pants. The sexy wrap is purposely designed to show the cheeks of her beautiful bottom whenever she bends forward. She bends forward often. The inside of her bronze thighs are smooth and full. When she sits, she keeps her slim thighs slightly parted. When someone looks interested, she opens a little wider.

I am stunned and completely aroused by her glowing beauty.

"This is my sister. Her name is Mandy." I manage to speak, but my voice is strained and my throat is tight.

"Oh Mandy, you are such a beautiful sister and you are in love. That is so wonderful!"

Mandy blushes and turns away, and I am surprised. How does the captain's daughter know that my sister has a lover? It is an awkward moment. No one speaks.

The playful princess snuggles her seductive body up against me and invites me to go for a swim. She is aware of my arousal and without waiting for my answer she runs across the deck and does a perfect dive off the side of the ship.

My dive dissolves into an awkward jump, and I make a huge splash when I hit the warm water. We come together in the water and Lila quickly unbuttons my pants and gives me a kiss on the chest as she goes under water to take a closer look.

Mandy watches her brother and the island nymph cling to each other in the warm clear water of the Caribbean Sea.

"I don't understand him, Bertha. He has a beautiful wife back in Ireland with a baby on the way and the fool is acting like a heathen. They are "doing it" right there beside the ship in broad daylight!" Mandy is pissed.

"I know Charles loves Shelly with all his heart. This so awful." She is sobbing. She wipes her drippy nose.

"Don't worry baby, this is nothing but runaway lust - it will pass. There is not a natural man on God's green earth who could have walked away from that temptation. It is just the way God made men. You just keep it your secret. Everything will work out just fine."

Bertha is mystified by Mandy's reaction to a spontaneous encounter of the flesh, especially after the way Mandy has been "carrying on" with Jack down in the cargo hold.

As evening approaches, the sun sinking low into the red glow of the western sky, the party winds down and people begin to leave the ship. There are twenty seven crewmen who have shore leave. Most of the sailors simply dive over the side and swim ashore. Some are invited to ride in island boats.

Mr. Games will not be leaving the ship until the next day. He has been assigned the "duty" by Captain Merritt. Jack is ordered to stay aboard as Officer-Of-The-Deck until eight o'clock the next morning. The young midshipman, and the two seasoned crewmen have been ordered to stay aboard and help Mr. Games keep the big ship and its cargo safe. The sailors are armed with muskets and the officer and the officer candidate have their pistols. Jack is wearing his Royal Navy sword, as well.

Captain Merritt departs for shore in his special boat. He is off to see his Island family. Three of his officers are in the boat, as well. There is something for everyone awaiting on this free love island.

The big ship is now eerily quiet, but I can hear laughter, singing and a rhythmic drum beat coming from the little village on the lush tropical island. The midshipman is standing on the bow of the ship gazing at the sunset and Mr. Games is smoking his pipe and slowly pacing near the helm - he and Mandy are softly chatting. There is a large ships bell hanging at the helm. In case of trouble Jack will ring the bell and the captain and crew will hustle back to protect the ship. The "duty" crewmen are sitting on deck near the entrance of the crew quarters. The two sailors are chatting and awaiting orders with muskets loaded and close at hand.

I am alone; high in the ship's rigging, looking over the open sea toward Ireland. My thoughts are of Shelly and I am trying to forget about Lila. I have a burning inside me and it is difficult to sort things out. The sex games, the captain's daughter and I played in the water, have piqued my desires, but left me a bit confused.

Mandy slips into a peaceful sleep in the officer's wardroom. She is awoken by a shake on her shoulder and she is shocked to see Bertha standing beside her.

"Bertha, I didn't think you ever came up here. Does Jack know you are up here?"

"Jack has gone ashore." Bertha just blurts it out.

"No he hasn't. Captain Merritt left Jack in charge of the ship." Mandy is sure about that.

"There is no one is on this ship except you and me." Bertha exerts.

I overhear their conversation and I yell. "Hey, I am up here!" I scramble down out of the rigging.

"Bertha says "Hello Charles," just like she has known me for a while, and I am sure I have never before seen her.

"Let's go into the Captain's cabin." Bertha is quick to take charge.

"We're not allowed in there." Mandy and I reply in unison.

"It's okay.. They will not be back until tomorrow morning, and then they will be too hung-over and too pussy-whipped to care about us." I can see Bertha has a way with words.

"First, I must find Jack – I know he is on this boat somewhere." Mandy's body is shaking with disbelief.

"No, he is not onboard. Jack went ashore as soon as it got completely dark!" I knew Mandy would take it hard, but I had to tell her.

"How do you know? Did you see him leave?" Mandy is pleading.

"Yes, I saw him. I was way up there in the crow's nest. I saw Jack go over the side and swim a lazy backstroke toward shore. The others followed him. We three civilians are the only people on this big ship right now. No one from the Royal Navy is onboard - just us."

I find it amusing and I admire Jack's spirit of adventure, but it is a serious violation of the British Navy's rules and regulations. Jack will be hung from the yardarm until he is dead, if he is caught disobeying orders and leaving the ship unprotected.

Mandy collapses face down on the Captain's couch. She is sobbing. "I thought he loved me, I hope the captain does hang him. He is such an asshole." she sobs.

In the meantime, Bertha is looking very regal and very relaxed in the Captain's chair. She grabs a bottle of Captain Merritt's private stock from the corner of the big oak desk. I sit quietly and admire her good looks and her confident manner as she pours three tall glasses of dark rum into HMS Cumberland's crystal glassware.

Bertha and I are in the mood for a drink, but Mandy is lost in her grief and she will not join us. We drink for a long while without any fear of being caught in the Captain's cabin. Bertha is happy and quite drunk when she looks at me and speaks seriously, "Charles, you should go ashore and see your pretty girl. She is waiting for you, and she always gets what she wants. It is impolite to refuse her. The island people will consider it an insult, and her mother will be angry with you. Go now and make her happy."

Mandy looks up and screams, "Yes, go! Go fuck her again! And, tell that fucking Jack to go to hell!"

I didn't know my little sister even knew that word, but it is all the encouragement I need. I slip over the side, climb down the rope ladder and dog paddle to shore.

Bertha rolls back the carpet behind the Captain's desk and pulls open a large hatch in the cabin floor. She deftly spins the dial on the captain's iron safe. It is obvious that she knows the combination. Bertha reaches down inside the safe and comes out with a heavy canvas bag. She tosses the bag aside and it clinks when it hits the floor. Bertha then begins to search through the files and the papers.

"Here it is!! I have it. I have it in my hand." Bertha is laughing and dancing around the room.

"This bag is full of gold coins and there is a little bag inside that is full of huge diamonds!" Mandy screams as she digs though contents of the bags.

"Yes, and I have the map to the hidden treasure right here. The pirates buried the treasure somewhere on Grand Bahama Island five years ago. Captain Merritt stole their map and some of the loot. It all belongs to Bertha now!"

"You had better put everything back Bertha – they will kill you for sure, if they find out you opened the Captain's safe."

"Don't you worry yourself one bit. Bertha will be all right. I'm leaving with this bag of gold coins and diamonds and I'm going to search for the buried treasure with this map." Bertha is moving fast now. She closes the safe and replaces the floor and the carpet.

She has put a little of the loot in a small pigskin bag and gives it to Mandy.

"Remember Mandy, if you say anything about this, they will arrest you for assisting me. They will torture you to find out what happened. You will be accused of helping me get away. Just hide this bag and say you were asleep. Keep your mouth shut and you will be safe. They will hang Jack and his crew of deserters for leaving their duty stations."

Mandy starts to cry again.

Bertha doesn't bother to say goodbye. She carefully tosses her big bag of coins and diamonds down to a man in a small boat waiting at the side of the ship. Quickly and silently, the boat disappears into the darkness. The Voodoo Priestess has prearranged her get-away.

Bertha's absence creates a vacuum on board the big ship. She executed her plan the minute the ship was left unguarded. She sent Charles away to make sure he was not a witness to the theft. She knew there would be turmoil and she didn't want to involve Charles in any way.

It is midnight and Mandy is left completely alone on the HMS Cumberland. She goes to her bunk, closes her door and cries herself to sleep.

I am the first to return to the boat. The dawn is cracking. First, I make sure Mandy is safe, in her bunk. Then, I check out the Captain's office. The office is clean and orderly with no sign of an intruder, so I go to my bunk.

"Bertha is back down in the bottom of the boat," I hear myself saying. I have no idea she has jumped ship with the all the captain's booty. Finally, just before the sunrise, I can hear Jack and his errant crew conversing out on deck. They are talking softly and laughing about their night ashore with the friendly island people.

I sleep; confident that all is well.

After four days of partying with the natives the captain announces that there is another ship on the other side of the island that is returning to Ireland. He encourages everyone to write a letter and it will be carried home by our sister ship. We, in turn, will carry their mail to America.

Mandy keeps walking around the galley saying, "I can't believe it."

"Can't believe what?" I finally ask.

"I can't believe that Jack did not get caught and fed to the sharks, and I absolutely can't believe that Captain Merritt has not discovered that his safe has been robbed." Mandy is whispering and looking nervously over her shoulder.

"We will just keep the goat's milk, and the cheese and eggs coming up from the bilge, so they will not suspect that Bertha has jumped ship. We can take turns feeding the animals, milking the goats and cleaning the bilge." It is a plan designed to give Bertha more time to get away.

"She is the nearest thing to a big sister I have ever had." Mandy muses.

After a week of rest and fun, Cumberland slips noisily out of the cove. Everyone is on deck waving goodbye.

The navigator plots a course for the Florida peninsula.

Chapter 4

America

Mercifully, we leave Mosquito Island after six days of rest and relaxation (Caribbean style). We are exhausted, hung over, and giddy. My gorgeous young Island Princess has completely drained all the marrow from my backbone; I am weak-kneed and limp as a rag. When I left her, she was smiling and eagerly awaiting the arrival of the next shipload of horny sailors.

My sister has made it her duty to remind me every day that I have a loving wife back in Ireland with a baby on the way. I know Mandy is right - I thank God for my beautiful Shelly. Shelly and Mandy and I have been instilled with the moirés of Ireland's Victorian society; none of which apply on Mosquito Island.

In an attempt to relieve my guilt, and save my eternal soul from the damnation of a burning hell, I seek out our ship's self-appointed chaplain. I confess my careless and adulterous behavior.

The 'Rev' clears his throat and begins to speak in his most pious tone. "I saw her, my son - that angelic female sex machine was put on earth by Satan himself, to remind us of the worldly frailness. You must pray every day to the almighty God in heaven for forgiveness. Go forth and sin no more." He sticks out a dirty hand, palm up. All I have for him is a big red apple that I swiped from the Captain's table. I give "his most holiness" the Captain's prized apple. In return, I get a big toothy smile of approval from the Rev. I feel better, but far from cleansed.

The next morning, the wind is howling through the rigging. It is still dark and a storm is brewing. I hang onto my hat and run for the galley with a fine rain stinging my face.

"Where are the eggs?" The cook is screaming.

"I'll go check." I reply calmly, reminding the cook to lower the volume. The captain is still sleeping.

My hands slide down the smooth rails of the ladder straight into the cargo hold. I am facing outward and my heels barely touch the rungs. When I return with a dozen large brown eggs, Mandy is setting the wardroom table. No one has arrived for breakfast, except Mr. Games. He is sitting at his assigned eating place, sipping coffee that he has served to himself. Mandy is giving him the "invisible" treatment.

"Does anyone suspect that Bertha has jumped ship?" Mandy whispers in my ear, as she takes a nervous glance over her shoulder.

"I don't think anyone has discovered she is gone. Let's be careful not to forget the eggs again or they will send someone down there to check on her."

"Yes, and it is getting a little stinky down there too. You need to go down to the bilge and do some shoveling."

Mandy changes the subject, "Do you think anyone knows that Jack left his duty station and went ashore unauthorized?" She whispers.

"No, no one knows - looks like he pulled it off. If the Captain finds out, Jack will go straight to the brig and be held in chains for a formal Captain's Mast."

"Then what?" Mandy smiles because she already knows the answer.

"They will hang him for sure." I say with a tone of finality.

Our big ship has finally reached American waters. The Navigator points toward the Florida Peninsula on our port side. We can see Grand Bahama Island off to starboard. The palm trees are blowing about in a gale force wind, and there is a warm peppering rain shower directly on our bow.

Captain Merritt and his first officer are busy studying the ocean charts in the Captain's cabin. Mr. Bloom, the first officer, is also the navigator. I serve the two senior officers coffee and biscuits while they formulate a plan to escape the foul weather. I listen carefully, but I don't understand much. I am struck by the formality of their conversation and the manner in which they address each other.

"The storm is building quickly, Captain. The barometer is in a free fall and the wind is increasing," the 1st Officer is obviously concerned.

"What is your recommendation, Mr. Bloom?" Captain Merritt always takes full advantage of his navigator's experience and expertise.

"Captain, we are heading directly into the path of a dangerous hurricane. The atmospheric pressure is falling fast; the wind is from true north now, thirty knots and building. As you know, sir, the cyclonic circulation of a hurricane is counter clockwise, so that puts the storm center well out in the Atlantic Ocean. It is northeast of our position and moving west, toward land and directly into our path."

"When and where will the storm reach the coast? Give me your best estimate?" The Captain has his own idea about the storm's movement, but he wants confirmation from his number one man.

"Captain, I forecast the storm will come ashore somewhere south of the Cape of Florida within 36 hours." Mr. Bloom does not hesitate to answer, but he leaves some room for error in his prediction.

The Captain doesn't speak, but his raised eyebrows indicate that he wants to hear more.

Quickly the navigator adds, "Sir, I recommend we immediately 'come about'. We should make our turn while the wind is still at thirty knots and head back to the South, Sir. We can find shelter in a cove on the lee side of Grand Bahama Island and ride out this storm secured at anchor. The island will afford good protection from the rolling seas and the big north wind that will surely blow well over 75 knots, Sir."

The Captain nods his approval and quickly gives two commands!

"Helmsman bring us about! Make our new heading 160 degrees. Hard to starboard", he barks.

"Mr. Bloom, plot a course to Dead Man's Cove." The Captain knows the island well.

With that, Captain Merritt hastily leaves the room. He is headed for the helm to execute the tricky 180 degree turn himself.

When a sailing vessel is headed directly into a strong wind, reversing course takes skill and experience. Mariners try to avoid 'coming about' when the wind is howling and the sea is rolling. During the turn, the direction of the relative wind shifts rapidly. Ship handling is extremely critical when the strong wind and the big waves are directly abeam and battering the vessel broadside. The sails, the rigging and the rudder must be skillfully managed to keep from being 'knocked down'. Then entire crew must function as a unit.

If a ship is knocked all the way over, it will most likely come right back up, but there will be damage; cargo always breaks loose, and sailors are often tossed into the turbulent sea.

Captain Merritt takes command. He rings the big bell; an order for all hands to 'turn to'. Sailors quickly appear on deck and assume their assigned tasks. Several acrobatic crewmembers climb barefoot high into the wildly swaying rigging. All the ships officers are shouting orders from the deck. Mr. Games climbs half way up the mainmast to help bring down a stubborn sail.

The Captain and his crew do a masterful job bringing Cumberland to a stable condition. She is now sailing with the wind and waves. She is heading back to the south and making good time.

Captain Merritt disappears into his cabin to help the navigator plot a course for safe harbor. The ship's officers and crew begin the job of trimming the sails – they are now, "running before the wind".

Cumberland must continue south for about ten miles before we can make our turn around the western tip of Grand Bahama Island.

It is a relief when we slip behind the Island. The sea calms and the winds lessen, but there is a haunting, hollow, howling sound that is unrelenting. The darkening sky has become alive with an iridescent bluish orange glow. There are flashes and streaks – all signs of a big blow.

Thankfully, the island has blocked the big rolling waves. Cumberland is 'steady as she goes', but there is a feeling of dread deep inside me I cannot understand.

Soon, we are approaching Dead Man's Cove. The entrance to the shallow harbor is narrow and lined with overhanging palm trees. After the anchor is set, the crew secures the rails of the big ship to palm trees on both sides of the cove.

HMS Cumberland is safely hidden from the raging sea and howling wind.

The Captain realizes it is right here on Grand Bahama Island, where the pirates buried the stolen treasure. He has the map tucked away in his floor safe. Captain Merritt rolls back the carpet behind his desk and opens the safe in the floor of his office. He fumbles to find the map. He is hoping to take a search party ashore and come back with the loot.

"Good God, I have been robbed!" The Captain is as white as the fluff on his shirt.

"My map is gone! My goddamn map is gone! The gold and my diamonds are gone, too!" He is screaming. "The safe must have been opened while I was ashore at Mosquito Island. Bring me that midshipman who was on duty with Mr. Games.

"Go down into the bilge and bring up that old nigger woman".

"Don't bring that black bitch into my cabin. Lock her in the brig." The Captain is shaking with anger.

I accompany Mr. Bloom down through the cargo hold into the bilge and, of course, there is no Bertha. She jumped ship with the Captain's booty eight days ago. Mr. Bloom notifies the Captain that Bertha is nowhere to be found.

"She must have slipped off the ship as we were pulling into Dead Man's Cove. She has probably taken the map with her and she is most likely searching the island right now for the buried treasure. We've got to catch her. We will go searching for her as soon as this blow is over. She can't do much digging in a hurricane." The Captain is pacing and trying to reconstruct the events leading up to the opening of the safe.

"How could she possibly open a safe or read a map? She's nothing but an ignorant animal. She can't even speak and she can't read numbers. I don't think it was she, sir." Mr. Bloom speaks. He has no concept of Bertha's abilities.

"I don't know. Maybe Mandy helped her. Mandy is in here every day, bringing me my fruit and coffee. I'll keel-haul that little red-headed Irish bitch and make her talk. Find her and lock her in the brig for safe keeping." The Captain is pacing and ranting.

Captain Merritt composes himself when the midshipman is brought in for questioning. The captain suddenly becomes aware that he has never ever even had a conversation with the youngster.

He is a chubby boy. His complexion is rosy and he has cherry red lips. Curly yellow hair covers his ears. He gives his age as seventeen, but he looks younger, much younger.

"How old are you, son?" The captain is truly puzzled.

"Seventeen, sir." The angelic boy lies. Just what the captain expected.

"How did you get assigned to my ship?"

"Mr.Bloom, your navigator, sir. He recruited me." The midshipman is fidgeting.

"Recruited you?

"Yes sir. He came to the marine academy and talked to the master and he talked to my mother."

"Where do you bunk?" The captain is sure he knows the answer to this one.

"In Mr. Bloom's cabin, sir." The midshipman looks toward the floor. Captain Merritt turns his head to hide a sly smile.

Captain Merritt directs the young cherub to sit across from him at the big oak table. He struggles to control his anger; he leans across the table and gives the boy a pat on the cheek.

"Tell me everything that happened when you and Mr. Games had the duty that first night at Mosquito Island. Remember, we were anchored on the south side and I went ashore? Tell me the truth, now, and I will let you go free, I promise." Captain Merritt is very convincing.

The youngster spills his guts in an attempt to save himself. He confesses all and begs for mercy with tears in his eyes.

"So…You and Mr. Games went ashore and left the ship unprotected." The captain's has his confession and his anger is starting to surface.

"Yes sir. I'm sorry, sir."

"Lock him up!' The captain yells to anyone in earshot.

The midshipman and Mr. Games are immediately put in chains. They are locked in the ship's brig together. The two sailors, also on duty that night, are chained to the mainmast just outside the brig.

Mandy is not implicated by the midshipman's testimony. She is seems to be off the hook, at least for now.

Mr. Bloom rushes to put in a good word for the boy. "Captain, I know the death sentence is mandatory for deserters, but you might consider a pardon for the boy. After all, he was not in a position to disobey his senior officer. Hang Mr. Games and make the boy watch him die"

I told the boy's mother, I would look after him, sir."

"Thank you, Mr. Bloom. I will sleep on your recommendation." The Captain is in no mood to show mercy.

Captain Merritt makes an entry in the ship's log. The Captain falsely documents in detail that the four deserters are condemned to death as the result of a formal Captain's Mast. The Captain does not bother with a trial, he needs vengeance and he wants it quickly.

Before the dawn, the very next morning, the condemned men are taken ashore in chains. When the orange tip of sun comes rising out of the Atlantic Ocean announcing the arrival of a new day, the four deserters are summarily and unceremoniously lined up and shot. The young Midshipman is pleading and yelling and struggling with his chains. The other doomed men are quiet and they keep their eyes down and their heads bowed. Mr. Games can be heard softly reciting the Lord's Prayer. The irons are removed from the bodies and they are buried quickly in graves already filled with water. One of the sailors is writhing and moaning; they just dump him in and cover him with muck.

Captain Merritt had ordered the four graves be dug the previous evening.

After the executions, the sun quickly disappears behind hurricane generated clouds, and we do not see sunshine again for three days. The wind is screaming and the rain is pounding. The big ship is resting securely in the shallow cove, ignoring the din.

Mandy is bedridden with grief. Her lover has been executed, and her only friend has jumped ship and disappeared, most likely forever. Mandy doesn't know she has narrowly missed being executed.

I was never a suspect and I think it was because I am not allowed inside the Captain's cabin.

Despite the horrific events, I am sleeping well. I already miss Jack. Jack and I were not friends simply because he was an officer and I am a lowly indentured servant working my way across the Atlantic. I know Jack liked me some, and from time to time he would confide in me. I often hoped he might one day become my brother-in-law. Obviously that had never entered Jack's mind. He stole my sister's affections easily. Mandy and I are completely trusting, of nice people. We are both wiser now.

The dawn is breaking. I roll out of my bunk and stagger out on deck for my morning pee. I poke my woody over the rail, and let go into the black waters of Dead Man's Cove. It is still dark. The wind and rain have finally subsided. It is warm and humid and there is a crescent moon reflecting off the water.

Suddenly, I sense that I am not alone. I can see rows of glowing white teeth and shining eyeballs all around the edge of the deck. I can smell people, wet people. When I reach the door to my bunk room, I am intercepted by two tall, muscular black men, with a large knife. My hands are quickly bound behind my back and they sit me down on deck without a word. As more sailors come out on deck, they too are apprehended and tied up – all without a struggle.

When daylight finally comes, there is a large group of Cumberland's manpower sitting in the middle of the deck immobilized; hands tied behind their backs and ankles bound.

There are over eighty Lucayan Warriors on board, along with some of their women and children. They are armed with knives and spears. The Lucayan Tribal Chief goes to the helm and rings the big bell. The clanging brings out Captain Merritt, the remaining officers and crew, as well as Mandy onto the deck. Everyone except the captain is tied up.

There is constant chatter and frequent outburst of laughter among the intruders. Captain Merritt talks to the chief and the chief talks back, but they cannot communicate. The chief is angry and very threatening, but no one can understand a word he is saying except when he yells, "Saint Augustine", and he yells it over and over.

"Does anyone speak this heathen's language?" The captain screams.

"Duff Green can speak it! Where's Duff? He knows these people. He lived here on Grand Bahama Island with one of their women for years. Go get Duff?"

They find Duff hiding in a storage locker and drag him out on deck. Duff is terrified. He is sure the tribe has come to kill him. His child and his woman are smiling at him. The warriors laugh loudly and let out a howl when they see their old friend, Duff.

Duff speaks to the captain. "Be careful Skipper, these bloodthirsty bastards are dangerous as hell."

"Ask him what he wants?" The captain replies impatiently.

"They want to ride with us to St. Augustine. The chief's teenage son was kidnapped and he is working in a slave camp up there. They have formed this war party to go rescue him."

"Tell the chief, we are sorry about his son and we will take them to St. Augustine, as soon as we have enough water under the boat to float her out of here."

The warrior's let out a big war hoop and the Chief throws both hands in the air and yells, "St Augustine!"

After a short conference with his officers, the captain speaks to the chief with Duff acting as the interpreter. "Chief, the ship is stuck in the sand. Your people must get off the ship so we will become lighter and float up; they can climb back aboard after we have floated free of the cove. The ship is too heavy to float off the sand with all your people on board – we must lighten up."

The chief doesn't understand ship handling. He thinks it is just a trick to get them off the ship and leave them stranded in the water doing the dog paddle. Seven of his warriors armed with spears surround Captain Merritt. Duff is horrified, he is gesturing and talking fast, but the chief is not buying it.

Then, without warning, Captain Merritt's limp body hits the deck. Just like that, the captain is dead – stabbed in the neck from behind. A fork tipped spear has severed his spine right at the base of his brain. The savage executioner and his cohorts let out a loud cheer.

They strip the captain's body down to his long silk underwear and tie him high on the main mast. His arms are straight out, crucifixion style. The chief orders the captain's body be facing forward so his spirit can help guide the ship. We are all horrified; watching in stunned silence.

"The chief wants a new captain to step forward". Mr. Bloom is the heir-apparent, but he is cowering in the back of the crowd. Under these circumstances, he doesn't want to be the Captain.

The chief and Duff are having a heated conversation. The chief is gesturing angrily and Duff is expecting to die at any minute.

Eventually, all the officers are untied and told to muster at the helm!

"The chief is going to pick a new Captain. He is looking for a man with big balls, so drop you pants – line up and give him a look". Duff Green is trying not to laugh.

The chief spots red-headed and petite Mandy in the crowd and motions for her to join the line-up. My sister resists until a grinning warrior puts a knife to her throat. Mandy smiles and he unties her hands.

The chief and a gang of his people go down the line looking closely at, and sometimes carefully touching testicles. Big balls are highly respected among the Lucayan people.

"Mandy yells at Duff, "What does the old bastard want from me? I don't have nuts!"

"He just wants to take a look at your breast. Please cooperate. He is in a killing mood." Duff is scared. So is Mandy.

The chief motions for my feisty sister to unbutton her shirt. "Hell no," she yells and tries to kick him in the shins, but the chief jumps back. Two warriors grab Mandy from behind and the chief reaches for her top button.

The instant he touches her chest, a thunderous and brilliant flash of lightning strikes our dead captain's body, hanging on the mast. It is a bolt out of the blue – there is not a cloud in the sky. The Captain's legs fly up and his head flops around and about. There is a lingering halo of white-hot fire circling the burnt body. The halo finally discharges off the top of his head with a loud pop.

Captain Merritt is smoking!

Mandy is blinded by the flash, she can smell burning flesh and she hears the Captain's crucified body making some spooky, grunting sounds.

When her vision returns, the chief and all his subjects are kneeling before her. Their heads are bowed and they are making a muffled, rhythmic, chanting sound.

"What the hell is going on here?" Mandy asks Duff who is picking himself up off the deck.

"They think you are a god. They think you commanded the lightning strike to protect yourself."

"Holy shit!" When Mandy yells out, the chief goes flat on the deck, spread eagle.

"The chief wants to know if he can stand," Duff is finally starting to feel more confident.

"No he can't stand, but he can sit. Have his murderous crew put their knives, spears and other weapons in a pile right in the center of the deck and untie our crew." Mandy speaks and Duff gives the order. The chief sits obediently with his legs crossed watching Mandy. He smiles nervously as the weapons are being surrendered.

Mr. Bloom quickly has all the weapons taken and locked safely inside a padlocked storage locker.

I approach my sister on my knees and whisper in her ear. "Please appoint me Captain of the Cumberland". Mandy likes the idea of me, her older brother, serving as the new Captain. Mr. Bloom thinks it is a great idea, as well.

It is settled. There is no swearing-in ceremony. I just make a dash for the Captain's cabin. I find the Captain's dress blues and don the big three-cornered hat. The blue jacket with its tails, trim in gold hangs a little loose on me, but I am looking good - I'm sure about that.

"Duff, tell the chief to have his men take down the captain's body." It is my first command as Captain of the Cumberland. I can feel the power and I like it."

After the body of our leader is laid out on the deck, Mr. Bloom brings out a silk burial sheath along with a large canvas body bag. The captain has carried these two items for over twenty years in the event he dies at sea, and it has finally happened – he's deader than hell and burnt to a crisp.

We put him in the sheath and the ships sail-maker sews him up inside. "Deep in the Arms of Jesus" is woven into the fabric on the front of the silk sheath. The encased body is then put inside the canvas bag, laced up, and laid over by the rail. When we reach the open sea the Captain's body will be committed to the deep. ('Committed to the deep' is a poetic way of saying 'dumped over the side').

I call a conference around Mandy – she is now our protector. First, I tell Mr. Bloom not to let me make any mistakes with the ship handling. He assures me, he will be right by my side. I make sure there are no warriors behind me and begin to explain my plan to the chief. I assure him that I will get him and his boys to St. Augustine.

The chief wants to see my testicles. I just ignore him. He is a little irritated, but when he sees Mandy glaring at him, he backs off.

"Chief you will need to gather food and fresh water for our three day journey to St. Augustine." I continue to use authoritative tones and I make my voice as deep as possible to assure him my balls are of sufficient size to command the big ship.

Mr. Bloom has advised me that we will be riding northward in the fast current of the Atlantic Gulf Stream and the wind will also shift to our tail as the storm center moves inland. We should make excellent time as we follow the coast around the Cape of Florida to St. Augustine.

It will be necessary to weave some long ropes to pull us out of the shallow cove. All the intruders must get off the ship, into the water and pull on the ropes. The chief is still skeptical, so Duff explains to him that they will then use the same ropes to climb back aboard. "No one will be left behind." Duff repeats over and over

Just making the ship lighter is all that is really necessary, but the chief understands the pulling part better. He reluctantly agrees to the plan.

The island people go ashore and bring back water, fruits and roots; provisions for the trip. A few warriors try to bring more weapons aboard, but these people don't wear many clothes, just loin-cloths, so it is easy to search them and confiscate any weapons. They bring long ropes they have woven from vines and hemp fibers (after we are underway, we will cut up the rope and smoke the hemp).

A large rusty cannon ball is placed in a special pocket at the foot of the Captains body bag. The big ball will assure the body sinks and the captain's hope was for his body to stand erect on the ocean floor and bobble along with the current.

The "Rev" presides over the ceremony and leads the crew in Captain Merritt's requested song.

Eternal Father, strong to save,

Whose arm hath bound the restless wave,

Who bidd'st the mighty ocean deep

Its own appointed limits keep;

Oh, hear us when we cry to Thee,

For those in peril on the sea!

The song has several verses, but this is all the crew knows.

The captain was not a devoutly religious man, so the Rev doesn't say much about the hereafter; he praised the captain as a 'leader of men' during his time on earth. "Amen, and farewell, My Captain."

When the body is slipped over the side of the ship into the emerald green waters of the Atlantic Gulf Stream, a loud disrespectful cheer goes up from the island people. Some of Cumberland's crew are misty eyed, but I don't see any tears.

The Lucayans are living and sleeping on deck; they are unsanitary, uncomfortable, sea sick and completely out of their element. They don't pay any attention to my commands, so I put Mandy in charge of making them go to the head when nature calls. She also makes them dip salt water up out of the sea and scrub the deck around them and keep things reasonably clean.

Everyone knows by this time that Bertha has jumped ship, so I assign a couple of the sailors to tend to the goats and chickens. "After the savages disembark in St.

Augustine we will have some fried chicken and barbequed goat." I promise.

Two days pass before we see the dim lights from the village of St. Augustine. We are miles off shore with our lanterns extinguished. Mr. Bloom navigates closer to the Florida shore. It is approaching midnight – the chief gives the order for his band of warriors to go over the side and swim to shore. You cannot hear or see them as they swim away, but there are tiny schools of glimmering light coming back to the ship. A half moon causes the ripples to glisten...

It is a bit strange, but I feel a little sad and alone when the warring party leaves the boat.

As soon as the savages are gone, everything changes. Mr. Bloom officially takes command of the Cumberland. Mandy is no longer a god. My three cornered hat and the blue coat, trimmed in gold, are rudely removed from my body and taken back to the captain's hanging locker. I am no longer the pseudo Captain of the Cumberland.

We continue northward along the coast. The day before we arrive in Savannah, Captain Bloom locks me in the brig. I am advised that I have been officially charged with the mutiny of the Cumberland, accessory in the murder of Captain Merritt, and impersonating an officer in the Royal Navy. These are trumped up charges, but someone must hang when a Captain in the Royal Navy is murdered.

Mandy is upset and scared. She is afraid to be alone with all the grubby sailors. She has a real need to be close to me, so she picks up an oar from the life boat and starts swinging it wildly at anyone in sight. She is screaming obscenities at everyone in earshot. One of the crewmen dances around in front of her and pretends to try and jump her, while a second sailor slips in behind my frightened sister and grabs her arms. She is quickly subdued and drops her not so deadly weapon. The brig door is cracked open a little and Mandy is shoved inside to join me in the small moldy cell. She lost the fight, but she ended up right where she wanted to be – next to me.

"Why was Charles arrested?" Mandy screams out through the bars.

"He took over the Cumberland and conspired to kill the captain." Captain Bloom is yelling back at her.

"Who says? That's incredible." I am yelling now. I was expecting an accommodation for my actions – and now this.

"I am bringing charges against you." Captain Bloom points a finger in my face.

"You lousy sack of sheep dung, you know it was the chief who murdered the captain and took over our ship." I am starting to realize that my stint as captain was not such a good idea.

"Well, that will all come out in the hearing. You will have your say. If it makes you feel any better, I intend to testify in your behalf." Captain Blooms knows how to work both sides of the situation.

"I don't trust you, you back-stabbing asshole." I am terrified. I am just 22 years old and I am being tried for murder the second time in my life.

There are several British ships in the harbor at the Port of Savannah. Justice is swift. One week after we arrive in Savannah I am taken to a ship anchored in the harbor to stand trial before a military tribunal. The Royal Navy Tribunal is made up of two young men in officers' uniforms and one older man in a powered wig.

After one day of testimony the gentleman in the wig announces: "You are wasting our time. It is obvious Captain Merritt was killed by savages; this boy didn't have anything to do with the mutiny or the murder. We will bring the savages to justice. Case dismissed!"

I am set free. The judge gets consistent statements from all of Cumberland's officers with no contradictions or conflicting testimony. In addition, the judge has just received a bulletin from St. Augustine; the chief and over forty of his tribe are in jail in Florida awaiting trial for war crimes.

The chief was captured with our murdered Captain's pocket watch hanging around his neck. Twenty seven of his warriors were killed in a futile battle and the chief was seriously wounded in an effort to free his beloved son from a life of slavery.

Mr. Bloom approaches me with his hand extended. "I hope you learned something from all this, young man."

"You can kiss my butt, and we are not getting back on your smelly boat." I do not shake his hand.

The next day First Officer Bloom is officially promoted to Captain Bloom. Bloom takes command of the Cumberland and Mandy and I watch as Cumberland prepares to set sail for the James River, in Chesapeake Bay, Virginia.

Captain Bloom knows that Mandy and I are required to serve as indentured servants to pay for our passage to America. Before we left Ireland, we signed an agreement to work in America and repay the debt. We were put in the custody of the now deceased Captain Merritt. Our new captain decides he is not responsible for our delivery to the officials in Richmond.

"The responsibility now lies with Charles. He must fulfill the agreement for passage and deal with his creditors or he will become a fugitive from justice." Bloom explains to his second officer over a beer.

Bloom has gained some respect for my ability to think fast and adapt to adversity, but he also feels I am too angry and too disturbed over the mutiny charges to try and reason with at this point, and he is right - I am pissed!

"As for Mandy, she has an innate ability to access a difficult situation and make the right decisions for herself." Bloom says.

Cumberland and her crew set sail for Virginia, leaving us in Savannah. They don't look back.

We are in a strange new land and all alone. I am weak kneed and flooded with a helpless feeling. We stand and watch as our home and our only friends sail over the horizon and out of sight.

"I've got to find a job quick or we will starve." I am thinking out loud.

"I have a surprise for you!" Mandy is wearing a big smile and her eyes are sparkling. She pulls out a little pigskin bag from under her dress.

I look inside. The bag is swimming with gold nuggets and gold dust.

"What's that fat little velvet bag I see inside there?" I'm shaking with excitement.

"Diamonds! Beautiful diamonds! Bertha gave them to me." My sister is proud and she is letting it show.

We are thousands of miles from home, but we are not broke. In fact, we are rich!

"If Captain Merritt had caught you with these, you would be in that hole on that island with a bullet in your heart." Mandy had taken an awful chance accepting the stolen gold and diamonds Bertha stole from Captain Merritt's safe.

We need food, clothing and shelter, so I measure out what I think is about two ounces of the yellow stuff and take it to the bank and I ask the teller to exchange it for U.S. currency. It takes the effeminate male teller an agonizingly long time to grade and weigh the gold dust. He finally gets it done just as a handsome pistol toting policeman enters the bank swinging a large nightstick.

I start out of the bank with a lot of cash in my hip pocket. The policeman extends his long arm across my path and stops me with a smile.

I am pretty sure the prissy teller has alerted this cop.

"Where did you get the gold, young man?" The policeman is talking to me, but smiling in the direction of the light-footed teller.

"Gold?" Now, I am sure that the teller has called the cops.

"My Dad gave it to me just before he passed on." I have never been a good liar, but the cop skips over my obvious fabrication.

"Where do you live?"

"We are on the way to Richmond, Sir." I worked my way around that question.

"With your wife?" The policeman asks.

"No Sir, It's just my little sister and me. We are planning to settle in Virginia."

"What is your name?"

"Charles."

Charles what?

"Charles McKenna, Sir."

"Charles, I have to complement you. You are the first Irishman that I have ever seen with money that wasn't drunk!"

"Thank you, Sir." I resist the urge to come to the defense of my countrymen.

"Believe me, I have seen a lot of Irishmen and the only sober ones have been the broke ones - until you. So, that says something for your character. Don't go flashing that cash and the gold around or someone will knock you over the head and relieve you of it."

"That sounds like good advice." I try to walk away.

"You got any more gold dust?"

"No Sir. Thanks for the advice, officer."

"Would you like to have dinner with my friend and me, tonight?" The policeman asks as he nods toward the teller. The teller is on his tiptoes, listening intently.

"No Sir. Thank you, Sir." I lower my head and head for the door expecting the policeman to order me to halt, but nothing more is said. The cop turns his attention to his friend.

Mandy and I check into the biggest hotel in town and go directly to separate bath houses to scrub our bodies with real soap and hot fresh water for the first time since we left home. The next day we go shopping for new clothes. We are flush with cash, so Mandy buys her first real purse ever, now she will have a more comfortable place to carry the gold and diamonds.

Everything we own is new except for the ivory broach that Mandy uses to commune with our dead mother. I still have the worn out pocket knife that I carry to honor my father's memory.

Mandy likes Savannah, but the people I have met, are a little weird.

That night, we put our new clothes over our bathed and powder bodies and go looking for a fancy restaurant on the waterfront. We have never ever been to an upscale restaurant. We are out of our element, but we manage to order a glass of fine wine from an uppity waiter.

Finally I accidently (on purpose) let the restaurant staff get a good look at my money roll. Everyone suddenly becomes very attentive.

"Isn't this amazing. They don't have any lamb on this menu at all." Mandy reads much better than I do.

We are talking about ordering some fried squid when I notice something familiar about a well dressed black woman with a large ornate hat being escorted toward a private dining room.

"My God, I'm almost sure that is Bertha!" I whisper to Mandy.

"And that is Lila for sure! She looks pregnant! They are going into a private room!" Mandy whispers.

"Lila who?" I pretend not to remember the late Captain Merritt's daughter or that I was intimate with her just a few weeks earlier.

"It's your over sexed girlfriend from the island and she is most likely carrying your child!"

"I don't think it could possibly be my child."

"Why not? The timing is right. We will ask her. She will know."

"No way that can be blamed on me. I was drunk and besides, I was just poking fun. I can't help it, if she took it seriously." My immaturity is showing through; Mandy finds my attempt at humor to be very distasteful.

"They were looking this way. Do you think they saw us?" Mandy's excited.

"I wonder if Lila knows that Bertha opened the safe and stole her father's fortune in gold?" Mandy is wondering out loud.

"I don't know, but whatever you do, don't mention it!" I give my sister a stern look.

We are trying to decide what we should do, when a man in a tuxedo comes to our table with a message, "You have been invited to join Ms. Lila in dining salon #2."

We are escorted to the plush, private dining room. There is silk on the walls and ceiling and a large slow turning fan hanging in the center of the room. Bertha does not look up until the waiter is gone and the door is closed.

"Look at you beautiful children!" She shouts. "You are all dressed up and so handsome."

"My God, Bertha! That is a gorgeous dress you're wearing! You sure don't look anything like a goat keeper." Mandy screams.

After things settle down a bit, Mandy, who is known for speaking out of turn, asks Lila the big question. "Is that my brother's baby you are carrying?"

Everyone is quiet until Lila answers shyly, "Maybe."

Bertha is quick to set things straight.

"It is Charles' baby for sure. Lila has already told me so."

Lila gazes uneasily into her glass of red wine and I just stare at my feet.

"Bertha always uses her black magic to see the future, children. I knew we would meet again. I just didn't know the exact time and place." Bertha is reminding us; she is a Voodoo Priestess.

Bertha starts to explain the overall situation to Mandy and me. She tells us that she found the buried treasure on Grand Bahama Island, so she is indeed a very rich woman, but black women are not expected to have money in America. So, Bertha is pretending to be Lila's personal attendant. All business and every transaction must be done in Lila's name. Bertha stays in the shadows, pulling the strings while Lila does all the talking.

Lila is carrying forged papers stating that she purchased Bertha at auction in the Savannah Slave Market. There are thousands of dollars in a bank vault in Lila's name. Lila will not go anywhere without her personal attendant.

"How did you manage to get this private dining room? Isn't it elegant?" Mandy asks.

"Negro's are not allowed to sit and eat with white people, so the man in the tuxedo put us in here for a small sum." Lila explains.

"America is a strange place," Mandy sighs.

The news that I am to be a father again has numbed my brain and locked my jaw.

Mandy feels she must tell Lila about her father's demise. She slowly and respectfully begins to tell Lila everything. Her father is dead and gone; murdered by savages and buried in the ocean depths.

The young Bahamian beauty is shocked when she hears her father is gone, but it is secretly good news for Bertha, because she knows that Captain Merritt would be looking for her to recover his stolen gold and jewels. Bertha says nothing, but she is deeply saddened and truly sorry for Lila's pain and sorrow.

After they recover from the bad news a bit, Bertha proposes a plan. We will ride the train to Richmond as a family. Bertha will produce a forged Bahamian marriage certificate for Charles and Lila and give them a Voodoo blessing.

"Charles will be the master of our little family and I will be his slave, attending to his wife's every need. Mandy will be the perfect little sister, just as she has always been. We must be very diligent and play our parts out carefully. We have gobs of money, so it will be great fun."

Bertha creates a forged document making Charles a slave owner and she scribbles out a fake marriage certificate for Charles and Lila.

"Why don't they just get married for real?" Mandy is being sarcastic.

"The church will not marry an obviously pregnant woman here in America." Lila warns.

"Well, that's the same as Ireland," Mandy affirms.

I decided to speak. "I will play this game for a while, but remember I am already married, and Shelly and my son are coming on the first ship leaving Ireland after our baby is born."

"I don't think you will ever see Shelly again – you should prepare for the worse." Bertha's tone is very compassionate and she is a Voodoo Priestess with mystical powers.

"Shelly is coming, soon." I am positively hopeful.

Lila shyly keeps her eyes lowered and I don't bother to look at my new pretend new wife.

"Bertha, how did you learn to write those forged documents?" Mandy changes the subject.

"I was taught as a child to read and write in English by the white lady my mother cooked and sewed for, and you can just scribble anything on a piece of paper and the Americans will accept it as legal – it's so easy it's scary. Mandy my dear, I could make you the Queen-of-Sheba with a single stroke of a pen," she laughs.

"Well, how did you and Lila get together? I didn't think she even knew you, Bertha" Mandy's pushing for an explanation.

"That night I left the ship at Mosquito Island, I found Lila hiding in the bottom of the row boat that came to pick me up." Bertha explains.

"Why were you hiding, Lila?" Mandy asks.

Lila doesn't answer.

"Lila's stepfather was making unwanted sexual advances, so she was forced to leave home." Bertha fills us in.

"He was always calling me a whore and my mother would not do anything. I think mother is afraid of him." There is pain in Lila's voice.

Everyone at the table was stunned into silence; finally Lila continues, "My brother was planning to kill our stepdad, so I left home to protect my brother." Lila is still looking at the floor.

"If your brother was planning to kill your step dad, it must have been worse than just calling you a whore." Mandy will not shut up.

"Yes, one night he was trying to rape me and my brother stopped him."

"How did your brother stop him?" Mandy has never cared for Lila.

"Enough!" Bertha yells. Everyone obeys and respects the generous and intelligent black woman.

After a long awkward silence, Bertha changes the subject. "Mandy, Lila and I saw the sailors execute and bury your boyfriend and three others on the island. What was his name?"

Oh, my god! You actually saw Jack die? Mandy is screaming.

"Yes, we were hiding in the sea grass. Jack was calm; he was praying. The youngster was begging and the other two were cursing."

"They shot them all."

"What were you doing out there during a hurricane?" I ask.

"We went there to search for the treasure. We found it. I had the map."

"We are very rich, but I need all of you to share the fortune with me. Next week we will ride the train to Virginia." Bertha is giving the orders.

Chapter 5

Train Ride to Virginia

The train station in Savannah is bustling. There are well dressed people with tickets in hand and their luggage stacked high in big wheeled carts. The noise around the busy train station is deafening. People are yelling, steam is blowing and bells are clanging.

Bertha looks like a rich lady's personal attendant in her freshly starched gray cotton dress that hangs down over her high button shoes. The big hat from the night before is gone. She is wearing a flowered sun bonnet and carrying a bundle of bags and boxes that belong to Lila. Bertha is wearing a leather money belt stuffed with greenbacks under her simple dress.

Lila is beautiful with her bronze skin, black hair and dark eyes. She looks like a young wife that can afford a slave to attend to her needs. Her shimmering green silk dress is full and flowing, but it makes no attempt to hide her pregnancy. The bulging money belt tied around her waist exaggerates her belly and she looks like she is carrying triplets.

I feel my new clothes have transformed me into a handsome something I am not; but I'm sure I can adjust. I easily come across as a wealthy gentleman in my dark blue tailored suit. I am wearing all the accessories that become a southern gentleman. A pigskin briefcase cuffed securely to my left wrist is meant to look like it holds big money; but in fact, it is a decoy, stuffed with paper. Like the others, I am wearing a money belt filled with large bills.

Mandy is very pretty in her blue silk dress. It hangs well below her knees with long black hose and black high-top shoes. She is carrying her new purse, but she has her cash, diamonds and gold dust in a belt around her thin waist.

Our attractive group of four is a walking-talking bank vault. We are escorted to a private compartment in the sleeping car. It has a locking door, a toilet and lavatory. The seats fold down for sleeping. I have a small pistol clipped to my belt and I am carrying a black bowler hat to protect me if I should get clubbed on the head.

There is a short knock on the door; the conductor comes in to see if we need any assistance.

"We have a place for your servant in the compartment behind the mail car." The conductor is addressing me.

"No thanks. She must be nearby at all times. My wife often gets the vapors." I explain.

"Well make sure she doesn't go walking about. This section is for whites only."

"That will not be a problem. She is never allowed to walk about."

Bertha doesn't look up, but she smiles when Lila pretends to come down with a slight attack of the mother-to-be vapors.

The conductor leaves quickly and gives the door a firm slam as he goes.

The door is quickly locked and the shades are pulled. Bertha assumes her position as group leader. She removes her sun bonnet and shoes and begins to speak.

"When we get to Richmond we will find us a nice plantation to buy. We will settle down as a family and grow cotton and tobacco and raise some livestock. And, I'm gonna find me a big black man to keep me happy!" She obviously has been planning this for a while, but it comes as a shock to the three youngsters. They manage not to comment. Mandy has visions flashing before her eyes, but she manages to keep her mouth shut, for a change.

When there is no reaction, Bertha goes on to explain; we will ride the train up the coast as far as Charleston and then spend some time in a hotel to rest and visit. The others would rather continue to Richmond without a rest, but they dare not disagree with the black woman who has declared herself leader of the pack.

The railroad has provided each passenger with a map of the route up the Southeast Coast of the United States. After Charleston they will go through Wilmington, North Carolina, on the way to Richmond, Virginia. Much of the terrain is swampy and the rails are supported by big timbers that have been driven at a slight angle into the shallow swamp. The timbers act to elevate the track above the swampy terrain for miles and miles at a stretch.

The wood burning locomotive certainly seems to be alive. It is belching smoke, sounding its whistle and bell, and churning its wheels; a hunk of black metal that is obviously possessed with a strong desire to perform. Bertha is afraid of all machines and she warns the others to show the big engine the proper respect or they will surely pay the consequences.

Bertha goes into a trance like state and prays to her Voodoo Gods for safe passage. In the Voodoo tradition she prays to soothe the soul of the big steam locomotive.

"I hope she doesn't sacrifice a chicken." Mandy chuckles an inappropriate remark.

Lila orders dinner be served in the compartment. The menu looks good and consists of chicken and ham with all the trimmings, but I decide to go alone to the club car for dinner.

"He is looking for companionship." Bertha understands.

"What? Doesn't that make you angry?" Mandy stares at Lila.

"No. He's just lonesome." Lila is unmoved.

"Why is he lonesome, he has you?"

"Don't worry little sister. He will be back." Lila doesn't seem to care one bit!

The dining car is deluxe with attentive and courteous servers. I have placed my order, and I am enjoying a glass of sipping whiskey when an olive skinned, dark haired, well dressed and well groomed young man approaches.

"May I join you?" He asks in proper English with a hint of an accent.

"Please, have a seat." I stand and point to the empty chairs. I turn to look for the dapper man's lady.

"I am alone. My wife has motion sickness and doesn't feel like eating." He senses my uneasiness.

"I am traveling with my wife and family – they are eating in our sleeping compartment." I explain at once just in case my new acquaintance is a sexual deviant.

"My name is Tony." He extends his hand.

"I am Charles McKenna, Sir." We shake hands.

Tony is looking at the briefcase strapped to my wrist.

"I know what you are thinking. There is no money in the bag, just important personal papers I am delivering to the Governor's office in Richmond." My explanation has been rehearsed in advance and it is designed to sound phony.

"You are Italian?" I ask quickly.

"Yes mostly, I was born in Sicily; however my mother's father was from Napoli in the South of Italy."

Tony raises his glass of wine toward me and proclaims, "Salute".

The Irish don't toast, we guzzle, but I raise my glass of rye and reply, "Cheers! "I'm Irish." I state the obvious.

"Yes, I know." Tony chuckles.

"And you are the best dressed Irishman I have ever encountered," he adds quickly, hoping I will not be offended by his levity.

We are two men from diverse beginnings and we enjoy a hearty dinner together. I feel I have found my first true friend in America.

I have some knowledge of Italy. I have known a few Italians in Ireland, but I have never met a Sicilian. I am very interested in learning more about Sicily.

"Well, it is a fairly large island off the toe of Italy," Tony begins, and the people are very friendly and very hospitable despite being mostly poor. If I took you home with me, my Mother would feed and pamper you, and my Dad would get you drunk on his homemade wine."

"Do they speak English like you?"

"No, we speak Sicilian at home."

"Is that sorta like Italian?"

"No, not much, but it is getting more and more like Italian every day."

After the tasty meal of chicken and shrimp, I start to fidget. I begin to look around the dining car.

"Let's go out on the back of the caboose and have a smoke. We might catch the sunset." Tony stands and offers me a cigar.

"Is this a Cuban cigar?" I inhale a delicious aroma.

"Yes. It is a Garbalosa. Do you like it?

"Very much. I must write down the name."

It is necessary to walk through the dark and narrow center aisle of the sleeping car to the caboose. Our shoulders touch velvet privacy curtains as we walk. We enter the caboose; the sun is strong and is bright.

Tony goes out on the caboose platform first. As I come through the door my new Sicilian friend grabs the briefcase strapped to my wrist and gives me a vicious blow to the back of my neck. The punch sends my Bowler hard hat flying and knocks me to my knees. My eyes are closed, but I can see stars. My left arm is painfully twisted and upward in an attempt to break the leather strap. The strap breaks. Tony loses his balance and falls back onto the railing clutching my briefcase to his chest. I am dazed and dizzy, but I manage to wrap my arms around his knees.

I stand up with all the force I can muster. The Sicilian bandit is half way over the railing already, so my quick move easily hurls my attacker over the rail and down onto the track. I pale with horror as his twisted body disappears into the distance.

Suddenly I am aware the conductor is standing next to me. "Stop the train!" I command.

"We are not going to stop the train for that thieving Wop," the conductor is spewing hate.

"He's not a Wop. He's Sicilian." Don't know why, but I wanted to get that straight.

"He ain't nothing now. You just gave that slick con-man what he deserved, I have watched him for weeks and he was always was up to something. I saw it all, and none of it happened. Keep your mouth shut and be proud of yourself for making the world a better place. Nothing will be said and he won't be missed. He intended to rob you and throw you off the train, so don't worry about him."

"Won't they find his body?"

"Not in this swamp. It is full of hungry critters – he will be crab shit by morning.

"What about his wife?"

"That's not his wife. She's just a little whore he pays to travel with him. I can handle her." The conductor is positive that if we keep it all a secret, there will be nothing to worry about.

I am dazed and a little wobbly. I stumble back to our compartment.

"Oh, my God! What happened? You're white as a sheet." Mandy yells. I fall into the room.

I am flat on my back on the floor and the room is spinning. My hand is on the back of my head. I feel a large lump rising back there.

Bertha notices the swelling is right at the base of my skull. She starts chanting in her native tongue. Mandy tries to help, but she paralyzed with fear. Lila sits and wrings her hands and tries to stay calm for the sake of her unborn baby. I am only half conscious. I vomit my shrimp and chicken dinner on the compartment floor. Bertha sends Lila for rags and a bucket of water.

The conductor notices the commotion and enters the room unannounced.

"I know what happened to him. I saw him fall back and hit his head on a chair in the dining room – drunk, I guess."

Bertha knows that the conductor is lying, but she doesn't know why.

Outside the compartment the 'little whore' starts yelling that her husband is missing, so the conductor goes out to muffle her.

"Don't let anyone see your master on the floor in that condition," the conductor instructs Bertha as he leaves the room.

She gives him the appropriate, "Yes sir, Capt'n", and then places my head and shoulders in her lap and does something very strange. She quickly smothers down my nose and mouth with her powerful left hand and simultaneously puts direct pressure on the sides of my neck to shut off my carotid arteries with her strong right hand. Bertha holds me tight until a clear liquid begins to run out of my ears. I begin to squirm desperately to shake loose from her vise-like grip. My face is covered with bright red and purple splotches and my eyes are bulging. I start to buck and kick, but Bertha holds on tight and the clear liquid continues to ooze out of my ears and the swelling on the back of my neck is relieved somewhat. I suddenly relax and go completely limp. This is Bertha's cue to release the pressure. When she releases her grip the clear liquid spurts from my nose and mouth. I take a big gasp of breath and I am coughing.

"Bertha, I thought you were going to kill me for sure." I gasp.

"Bertha just saved your life, Charles; you're going to be all right now." Bertha brags.

"Was that black magic?" I could barely hear.

"Bertha spent many years studying to become a Voodoo Priestess. It is not magic, it's medicine. You rest now. You will be very weak for a while."

Mandy is too scared to speak, but finally she recovers her senses and asks Bertha how she knew what to do. Berta explained that her departed mother and her dead grandmother were present and they were advising her during the episode.

"They were both here. I could hear them as plain as day. Mama was guiding me and instilling me with the confidence to act forcefully."

"What was that water coming out of his ears, nose and mouth?"

"It was his spinal fluid. The blow to the back of his head caused the fluid to spill into his brain and forcing out the life giving blood."

"Holy Moley!" Mandy exclaims quite inappropriately.

Lila crosses herself and says nothing. I fall into a rhythmic breathing pattern. I start to snore a little. They put a pillow under my head and leave me on the carpeted floor.

Slick Tony's companion, the little whore, is scared and all alone, and screaming her head off.

"We may have to dispose of her too," the conductor whispers in my ear.

I can't open my eyes, but I can hear him. I am not prepared to dispose of anyone.

"We've got to get rid of her. She is going to scream and yell until she causes an investigation," the conductor warns.

Mandy takes over. The working girl's name is Rose, and she and Tony are not married, just friends. Rose quiets down and quits shaking when Mandy hugs her and talks to her softly.

I recover enough to call a meeting of the family. I explain to the group that I threw Tony, Rose's friend, off the back of the train in an act of self defense. The conductor is convinced we should keep Tony's demise a secret, but Rose has become a problem.

Mandy quickly proposes that we simply take Rose into the family and care for her.

"Rose didn't really care for Tony. She just needed someone to take care for her. If we take her in, she will calm down and keep quiet." Mandy says.

"Well then, that's what we'll do?" I look to Lila and Bertha for approval. They nod in agreement.

The incident is over - finis. No one ever reported Tony missing.

The stop in Charleston is a good rest for our group. We all go and do some shopping for Rose, and then enjoy some fancy dinning and hot baths. Mandy insists that her new friend share a room with her. Rose is more than willing to be Mandy's bed buddy.

Rose proves to be an easy person to have around. She is smart and industrious. She has an eye for men and she tries to fix Mandy up with a young good looking guy in Charleston. Mandy is almost sixteen now, but she is not interested in pursuing any male. In fact, Mandy gets irritated and upset when anyone even talks about finding her a boyfriend. Needless to say, Rose finds that a little strange until Lila explains that little Mandy was brutally raped when she was just eleven years old and her first serious boy friend was tragically executed.

"Jack was shot and buried, by order of my father, Captain Merritt. He was buried on Grand Bahamas Island." Lila is not apologetic.

The trip on up to Richmond Virginia is scenic and uneventful...

Chapter 6

* *

The Plantation

Mandy and I are arrested as we step from the train in Richmond. Local officials meet the train in Richmond and promptly take us into custody. We sold ourselves into servitude before leaving Ireland. We now have an obligation to work as indentured servants and pay our passage across the Atlantic Ocean to America. I am no stranger to incarceration and Mandy has been in jail before, also.

We are no longer poor. In fact, we are flush with cash. We are eager to start a new life in the new world and that doesn't include being someone's slave. Mandy suggests that we simply dig into the money belts and buy our freedom outright, but I don't trust the jailer. I insist we keep the money and gold dust safely hidden under our clothes until Bertha arrives.

Lila shows up in a dither at the slave trader's office and offers cash to buy our release from bondage. Bertha is right beside Lila, calming her and giving her advice.

"Whatever they demand, you offer a little less than half," Bertha whispers to Lila.

The negotiations begin. After an hour of haggling, our happy little family leaves the jail free and clear, with the proper documents in hand. We find a hotel and settle-in. Bertha is allowed to accompany Lila in her room during the day, but the hotel has special sleeping quarters for Negro servants. Mandy and her new found friend, Rose, share a room. I have a room with an adjoining door to Lila, but I am pretty sure that my pregnant, pretend wife is not interested in sleeping with me. I resist the urge to knock on her door.

Bertha cooks up an ambitious plan. She intends to search for an established, fully operational plantation and make it into our new American home. She needs everyone in the family to help implement the plan since Negros' are not allowed to own property in America.

We are lucky - we find 12,000 acres of gentle rolling land with a large, but slightly run down, house. The house is big, fully furnished, and structurally sound. There are two large barns complete with animals, carriages and farm machinery, in addition to several out buildings, fenced pastures and large cleared fields already filled with crops. Bertha gives me money; I put it in the bank and the plan is to pay in total with a check.

My role as Master of the family is to do all the negotiating. Even though everyone agrees the asking price is reasonable, we will try to buy it for less. All five family members are in the room during the negotiations.

The bickering starts as soon as we sit down together. The present owner's attorney finds out at once; negotiations will be difficult. He quickly becomes agitated, angry and impatient.

"Why do you always look at that old nigger woman before you talk?" The lawyer has a disgusting tone. He is rude and disrespectful, but I am determined to remain calm.

I think he has figured out that black Bertha is actually running the show?

In the end, we manage to purchase the plantation for much less than the asking price. It required three days of haggling because Bertha insisted I maintain a firm, stubborn negotiating posture. She kept reminding me that money talks and we have the cash.

During the transfer of the deed and the disbursement of funds the attorney is outwardly angry and resentful. We have never seen the actual owner of the property.

"How did a 'wet behind the ears' Irish boy manage to negotiate such a good deal?" The attorney feels defeated and he apologizes to his distressed client. "If you weren't so desperate to get rid of the place, I would have told them all to go to hell."

After a short pause for some reflection the attorney continues, "There is something smelly about this bunch. Sure, the boy looks like a nice young man, but he is as uninformed as a fence post. I am positive he was being coached by his slave woman, even though the black bitch never said a word. His main negotiation tactic was to make a low offer, ignore our counter, and then just get up and go back to his hotel without saying a word. It almost drove me nuts. I checked with my brother-in-law at the bank, and I know these people have plenty of money. They could have paid our asking price with ease. Where the hell did an uneducated and unsophisticated family of youngsters get all that money anyway?"

"Keep your eye on that 'Black Mammy'. Something's fishy here. It will come out eventually. You can bet on it!" The attorney is waving his arms and his face is flush and his eyebrows are twitching.

The seller of the seemingly perfect plantation is glad to get rid of the property at any price. He has been unable to go back into his house since his wife and two children died there; ravaged by small pox.

"Now that the deal is closed, I think you should tell them the place is infected with the smallpox." The seller suggests to his attorney.

"That is not our concern – let them all get the pox and swell up and die." The lawyer is a disturbed man.

So… We move into the fully furnished big house and everything seems perfectly beautiful.

Bertha's first order of business is providing a male companion for herself. She has plans to purchase a big black buck to keep her happy. Technically the black man will belong to me, but in reality he will be Bertha's sex slave. I reluctantly agree to go down to the Shockoe

Bottom district with her. We will look for a candidate for the job of 'filling her needs'.

Shockoe Bottom, the infamous slave auction district near the James River, is bustling with a collage of humanity. People are already rushing about the cobbled streets when we arrive in our new one horse carriage. I am trying to look the part of a southern gentleman, and the well dressed black Bertha stays close by my side. She pretends to be attending to my needs; at one point taking a kerchief from her purse and wiping the dust off the toes of my shiny black boots.

Red flags are flying on the doorways where auctions will be held that day and there is a list and description on each door of the slaves that will be offered for sell. Of course, we are bargain hunting. We plan to use the same discreet signals during the slave auction that worked so well during our previous negotiations and acquisitions.

I feel out of place and uneasy, but no one seems to notice us when we enter the first auction room. Bertha steers me directly to a tall, muscular black man who looks to be about thirty years old. I ask him his name and he says nothing. Bertha asks in French and he replies, "Dandridge".

Dandridge is wearing nothing but a white loin cloth that is wrapped up though his crotch and around his waist with the excess hanging down between his legs halfway to his knees. She signals to me her approval and whispers that we should check his privates. I am mortified at the thought, but I call the slave trader over and ask if we can take him into a private room for the inspection of his genitals. The dirty white man in a tattered black suit and high-top hat speaks to Dandridge in French.

The slave disrobes right then and there. Bertha is pleased with what she sees at first, but then she notices that Dandridge has no testicles. I turn away and motion for the big black man to cover himself.

"What happened to him?" I don't really want to know.

"He was castrated by a previous owner, so he could work inside the big house around the white ladies. It makes him a prized nigger, Sir."

I look at Bertha, and then I explain to the slave trader that we want a big buck, capable of breeding.

"Well now, that's different. You come back at eleven o'clock and you can take a look at Frank."

"Let's look at Frank now. Where is he?" I assert.

"He is in that room over there fucking a young filly right now." The dirty man points at a door across the room.

"What?" I am embarrassed, but Bertha laughs out loud.

"A pregnant bitch will bring more, especially if we can say she is carrying Frank's baby," the white man explains.

"Can we see Frank now?" Bertha is excited. She knows she should not talk business.

The slave trader looks angrily at me, "Don't allow your slave to address me, I don't negotiate with niggers."

"Can we see Frank now?" I repeat in Bertha's exact same tones.

"Sure! Follow me."

The slave trader opens the door and it is obvious that Frank has all his parts, and by the look of ecstasy on the young slave girl's face, his parts are working really well.

Bertha walks around the room and takes a good look from every angle.

"Let's talk price." I have seen enough, but Bertha whispers to me that she wants to talk to Frank one on one before they begin to negotiate price.

"Well, he will be in there for a while longer, she is not going to let him get away as long as she can keep getting him up." The white slave trader grins.

"We'll come back at eleven." Bertha blurts out again. I am shocked by her obvious excitement.

The slave trader looks disgustingly at me for confirmation. I shake my head in the affirmative.

"Why do you need to talk to him? You saw him in action." I ask, as we walk outside.

"Yes, I sure did see some action. I admire his strong beautiful body and sexual prowess, but I need to look into his eyes and search the depths of his inner self. If his heart is half as dark as his black ass, we will just have to find another man for Bertha. I want a big powerful man, but his soul must be clean and pure." Bertha sounds like she is making a joke, but I quickly realize she is very serious.

"Damn it Bertha. I don't understand all this."

"That's because you're young and white, Charles. Everything is going to be just fine, baby."

We go back at eleven and Frank passes Berta's *in depth* personality check with flying colors.

She feels she has found a good and honest man with the physical attributes she is looking for. Frank is scheduled to go on the auction block that very afternoon, so we forego negotiations and pay full price for him.

We remove Frank's handcuffs and leg irons and he jumps into the back seat of the carriage. He is rubbing his wrists and ankles, but he seems happy.

On the sunny ride into the country and home I talk to Bertha and let her know that I think slavery is a disgrace to mankind and I don't like her pretending to be my slave, and I sure as hell don't like being Frank's master.

"All those white heathens down there by the river are going to burn in hell for what they are doing to their fellow human beings!" I feel the need to say it out loud. I want everyone in Richmond to hear my grievance.

Bertha senses that the 'inhumanity of man' is starting to wear me down.

"You were raised in the protected all white environs of a small village in Ireland and the workings of this new world are beginning to shock your system." Bertha is truly wise.

"Hell Bertha, I haven't been protected from anything. I am a very young man, and to my great regret, I have already killed two men. I have traveled half way around the world. I have a pregnant wife in Ireland and a pregnant girlfriend here in America, and I started drinking hard liquor on a daily basis when I was twelve years old. I have not lived a shelter life by any standard."

"Well, the first man you killed raped your little sister and you were insane with rage, and the second man you 'sent to hell' tried to rob you and throw you off the back of a train. He hit you so hard on the back of you pretty neck that you would have died for sure if Bertha had not been there with her Voodoo medicine to save you. Many good and decent men have to kill another human sometime during their lifetime; you just got an early start, that's all, baby. You were very much protected in your younger, more formative years. Most men your age have several children already and all good men have more than one woman. Women cycle and men don't. It is unhealthy for a man to go without; he could explode if he goes too long without a woman. Drinking just makes it easier for you to commune with your God and visit with the spirits."

Her little talk makes me feel better about myself even though everything she says conflicts with my Methodist upbringing.

Bertha is the nearest thing to a mentor I have ever had and she has made me feel better about being a murderer, an impregnator of two women at nearly the same time, and a disciple of the demon rum.

"You should go to your little woman tonight. Lila will give you the comfort you are in need of."

"Won't that hurt the baby?"

"No, just don't you get too frisky, and let Lila lead the way. The baby will be fine." Bertha is pleased by my concern for the unborn child.

The next morning Lila and I arrive late for breakfast. We are holding hands. I am very attentive to my pretty lady. Lila is smiling and happy. She begins to comb out her long, shiny, straight black hair and tell Bertha about the baby. "He is rolling around and kicking me hard."

Frank enters the dining room balancing a big pan of hot biscuits up over his head on his huge muscular right arm.

"Gracious! Who is that?" Lila is amazed by the enormity of Bertha's big man.

"I'm Frank ma'am. I'm Mr. Charles' nigger."

"Well, he works for me in the daytime, but he belongs to Bertha at night." I want to get that straight.

"You just call me Lila." She makes it sound like an order and it brings a concerned look from Bertha.

"Yes Ma'am, Frank will call you Lila for sure."

Bertha leaves for the kitchen and brings out a huge plate of ham and eggs and she and Frank disappear back into the kitchen just as Mandy and Rose stagger into the dining room looking a little desperate for a cup of coffee.

Rose and Mandy are both 5 foot 2 inches tall and they weigh exactly the same (105 pounds). They like to share their clothes and they agree on style and color-almost always.

Rose, with her olive complexion and straight black hair, contrasts completely with Mandy's curly reddish blond hair and fair skin with freckles. They were each raised without a mother's love. Neither has had much formal education. Both young ladies are above average in intelligence and each has acquired plenty of practical knowledge at a young age. The two girls share a good work ethic with personal intensity and a strong will.

They follow the aroma of brewing coffee into the kitchen and find Bertha and Frank playing and laughing over by the red hot, wood fired, cook stove.

"Frank and me was married last night! We had a Voodoo wedding and I wrote us out an almost legal marriage certificate." Bertha boasts.

"What? You married him the same day you met him? Why didn't you invite us? You know I love weddings." Mandy is completely amazed.

"Well. All the guests at our wedding were from the spirit world. My Mama and Grandma were there and I put Frank in a hypnotic trance, so he could see his Mom and Dad for his first time ever."

"Did you kill a chicken?" Mandy never misses a chance to bring up the chicken ritual.

"Don't you make fun of me child, I'll put a Voodoo curse on your skinny ass." Bertha is in a happy mood.

"Welcome to the family, Frank – I'm Mandy and this is Rose."

"Pleased to make y'all's acquaintance Ma'am."

"Come see me anytime, Frank!" Rose smiles and extends her smooth little hand.

"You forget about Frank, you lusty little bitch, he's my husband." Bertha's eyes are flashing and her happy mood has disappeared.

"Sorry, I was just kidding." Rose is surprised and a little frightened by Bertha's outburst.

"Oh, that's alright, baby. Bertha just hasn't had a good man for a while. I'm sorry I yelled at you."

"That's fine. I understand." Rose doesn't intend to cross the boss.

Mandy and Rose are together day and night and Mandy has never been happier. They go back into the dining room and sit down to a hot breakfast of eggs, ham, grits, milk gravy, fried apples, home baked bread and fresh milk and coffee. After the newlyweds get everything on the table, they sit down to eat with the family.

It is a new experience for Frank and he is very ill at ease eating with white folks. Bertha manages to calm him down after a bit. He devours six eggs with all the trimmings and leaves the table looking for some more butter for his hot biscuit.

"Where did you get the cold fresh milk?" I had expected buttermilk.

"It came right out of our 'spring house' chilling room. I guess it was the Colonel that built that thick walled, stone house right over a clear cold spring, and it is located just outside the door, right behind the kitchen."

The cold, fast flowing spring water running through the little stone building keeps everything cool, so the milk and butter and other food stuff comes out well chilled, crisp and fresh.

"They used rock to build the 'spring house' because the thick rock walls keep the summer heat out. They also picked this spot to build the big house because it is close to the big spring and you need a cool place near the kitchen to store food." Frank lectures as he starts clearing the dirty dishes.

"Never mind the dishes, Frank. We have to go to town today and mail some papers. Hitch that pair of matched, chestnut gelding's to the day carriage and get us ready to travel in style."

"Yes suh, Mr. Charles."

"Frank, please just call me Charles and drop the sir and mister." I am pleading.

"No. Frank can't do that." Bertha interjects herself into the conversation.

Bertha takes a long time each day explaining to the family group that each of us must play out our roles in the big pretend family, if we are going to be permitted to live in the culture of the American South.

I must pretend to be a southern gentleman and plantation owner and I must pretend to be Lila's husband even though I have a wife in Ireland. Lila is going to have to learn the ways of a southern gentleman's wife and when in public, she must talk down to her Negro servants. Mandy and Rose can be themselves (ladies with close lady friends are well accepted in the South), but they must remember to treat Bertha and Frank and other Negro's as the underclass. Frank knows how to be a slave; he was born into slavery. Bertha is rich and feisty and she sometimes reluctant to play her part.

"Well, I'll do it, but I don't like it." I grab another hot biscuit and head for the bath house to clean up.

When I come out, all washed and clean shaven, Frank is waiting in front of the house with the team of chestnut geldings harnessed to the carriage and tied to the hitching post in the front yard. I untie the team, and jump onto the spring supported carriage seat and Frank commands the team to move out. I don't know much about driving a team of horses, so Frank gives me some basic instruction on the way in to town. I take the reins; it feels natural to me.

"You sho' have a special knack for horses, M'asr Charles, Sur."

I give Frank a dirty look, but we remember Bertha's lecture and we look at each other and smile.

The Post Master has heard about me already, and he knows we have purchased Colonel Davis' plantation.

"How you plan to get the small pox out of that big house?" The postmaster speaks though the window of wooden shack post office.

"Small pox! What small pox?" I'm shocked and Frank is turning a little white.

"Hell, the pox killed his whole damn family and the Colonel his self was sick as a dog for two months. They didn't tell you about all that? The Colonel's old lady and their two kids died right there on the place with a scathing fever. The Colonel wanted to burn the house right down to the ground, but that slimy lawyer talked him into selling it."

"How do you spell your last name?" The postmaster is back to the business of finding my letter.

I am stunned. I can't answer the postmaster's question, until I am asked to spell my last name for a second time.

"I'm Charles McKenna, sir. It's M-c-K-e-n-n-a.

"Did you just come over here from Ireland?"

"Yes Sir."

"I know I have a letter for you back here somewhere. It came over on a boat a couple of weeks ago. I almost threw it away, but it was marked urgent."

"Here it is!" He smoothes out the wrinkles and gives it to me.

I just fold it up and stick it in my hip pocket. We leave without further comment.

Our horses are brought to a trot and we are almost half way home when Frank asks, "ain't you gonna read the letter, Mr. Charles."

"I can't read handwriting much at all. I'll just let Mandy read it to me."

"Excuse me for asking, sur. But if you can't read handwriting, what can you read?"

"I can read the newspapers and books and other printed stuff pretty good."

"Can you write?" Frank is digging to see how far he can go without pissing his new master off.

"I can sign my name really good." I brag, without getting even a little bit pissed.

"Oh, yes sur. Well I'm pretty good at looking at the pictures in the newspaper and figuring out what is going on sometimes my own self. But, I just puts down a 'F' when I signs."

"Well, when I saw you in action down at the slave market the other day, you could put down a 'F-F' for 'Friggin-Frank'." I laugh a little too loudly and little too long at my own crude joke. My laughter makes Frank uneasy.

"Oh, no sur, that slave-trader made me mount that little bitch. I didn't want to do that. No sur!"

"Well, you had warmed up to it pretty good by the time I got in there. That's for damn sure! How old was she, anyway - about sixteen?"

"Yes sur, she was a youngun' for sure. But, she was haired-over real good and she already had some pretty good little titties." Frank has his standards.

"You are a big man, Frank. How did you manage to get inside her, anyway? Didn't she scream and cry with pain?" I am genuinely curious and I am thinking about my own little sister that got horribly raped."

"Well, the bitch say she like *some* pain, but I didn't want to hurt her too bad, so I rubbed her up some and kissed on her sweet spots real good before we got it started."

"Did she like it?"

"Yes sur, four times she did. She cried when I was leaving, and she said that there must be something wrong with me!"

"She thought there was something wrong with you?"

"No, she thought something was wrong with her – she thought she was just not sweet enough for me."

"Young girls sometimes just don't know yet - a man gets 'pussy whupped'. Even a good man after three or four times."

I am too shocked to answer, so Frank continues.

"But now, I learned about getting girls 'ready' from my big sister – yes'sur, she taught me all about that."

"You're not supposed to do that with your sister." I am amused.

"Well, she was actually my half sister or maybe my cousin or something, and I was just a little boy."

I replay our conversation over and over in my mind and I smile the rest of the way home.

Our dysfunctional, make believe family, has just learned by a chance conversation with the postmaster that our newly purchased plantation's 'big house' is infected with the small pox virus. Something must be done; something decisive! And, it must be done right away.

Bertha makes a painful decision to remove everything from the house that is not nailed down and burn it out in the cow pasture.

"Mandy, you and Rose get Lila out of here right now. Take her back to the hotel and stay until we come for you. We don't want anything to harm that baby in her belly."

"We will start carrying stuff out of here as soon as you leave. Rose you drive the carriage; and Lila, I have some cash for you and Mandy."

Bertha always leaves Rose out when she disburses money; she lets Mandy take care of Rose. She wants Rose to become completely dependent on Mandy for support. Bertha is happy for Mandy. She has found a companion to help smooth over the scars of her abused past and the awful rape.

"Rose is basically a good girl. She has no family, so she became a whore to survive." Bertha explains to Frank.

"Yes'um." Frank doesn't have the slightest idea what Bertha is talking about. He assumes that all women are whores and he doesn't think anything is wrong with that.

Bertha orders the bed coverings, mattresses, drapes and rugs, be brought out of the house first. Frank starts a big pile in the cow pasture - upwind of the house and clear of the trees and brush. We find a three gallon, greasy can of coal oil in the equipment barn. Frank douses the big pile of furnishings generously to get the fire started quickly. The flames begin to pop and leap upwards and soon there is a thick column of black smoke rising high into the clear blue, afternoon sky. Neighbors and people passing nearby see the smoke and come to investigate. A crowd quickly gathers around the perimeter of the fire. It is a big blaze, engineered to hopefully eradicate all the small pox germs.

I quickly hire several big boys from the crowd to help move things out into the pasture. The house is being emptied quite rapidly. As soon as a room is empty, Bertha starts scrubbing the floors and walls with hot lye water.

Outside, our neighbor, Colonel Jones, makes a majestic arrival. His big steed floats gracefully into the flickering light of our leaping fire. The colonel is riding his favorite buckskin stallion. Two large white dogs complete his entourage. The dogs stand obediently in the firelight, ignoring the excitement, and awaiting the colonel's next command.

Colonel Jones quickly moves through the pile and inspects the furniture from the master bedroom, the dining room, the library and the main entrance foyer. Fine cherry and mahogany hand crafted furniture is being carried out of the big house and deposited very close to the fire. Colonel Jones is thankful he has arrived in time to save these historical pieces. He stands guard with his swagger stick and sends Frank to fetch Mr. Charles McKenna

After the customary greetings, the Colonel expresses his strong desire to save certain furniture from the inferno.

"All these pieces in this area were once the property of former President Thomas Jefferson," he points with the swagger stick. "Please don't destroy them, Sir!"

I have never heard of Thomas Jefferson, but I am glad I don't have to burn the elegant furniture. Colonel Jones is pleased when I agree to save the specified pieces from destruction. The Colonel suggests that all the upholstery and the stuffing be ripped away and burned.

"If the furniture is indeed harboring small pox it would be in the cloth and in the stuffing." Colonel Jones is an educated, intelligent man.

The cloth upholstery and stuffing is ripped off and thrown into the fire. The wood frames are then taken to an out-building and stored for pick up later by the Virginia gentleman and our friendly neighbor.

His mission accomplished; the Colonel mounts his big horse, salutes the crowd smartly with his swagger stick, and commands the muscular bundle of nervous power that is twisting and dancing between his legs to head for home. He whistles loudly for his dogs. The obedient canines come running. They gallop closely behind the Colonel. The big dogs are playfully nipping at the rear hoofs of the big horse as they leave the glow of the fire and disappear into the night.

The cleansing fire burns all night. It is still smoldering at sunrise. I have not slept for hours, so I crawl into the hay barn with a jug of whiskey and sit down exhausted, dirty and covered with smoke stains and soot.

When I wake with the morning sun in my face, I remember the letter from Ireland. It is stuck deep down in my back pocket. The letter is hand written, but it is printed. I read it slowly:

Dear Charles McKenna,

I regret to inform you that your dear wife, Shelly and your newborn son, both died as the result of a difficult childbirth.

They had a proper funeral and it was well attended.

Sincerely,
Thomas O'Malley

I am stunned and finding it difficult to breath. I read the letter over and over with a big swig of whiskey between each read. It is too tragic for me to comprehend. I cannot bring myself to believe my loved ones are dead. Finally and mercifully, I pass out; drunk in a bed of hay.

Bertha is frantic when she finds me unconscious and lying in a swill of my own vomit and urine. The crumpled-up death letter is gripped tightly in my left hand! She sends Frank to town to bring Mandy home.

Chapter 7

* *

Revenge

Mandy and Bertha grab me under my limp arms and drag me head first to the bath house. They remove my putrid clothes and put them into a black iron pot of boiling water. Frank lowers me into a big wooden tub of warm water. Bertha cooks up a mixture of Voodoo medicine to help me recover from my massive intoxication. They force me to swallow a big spoon-full of the black mush and then stand back as I hurl it out of my gut and over the side of the tub. After three regurgitated doses, I recover enough to fight back. I refuse to take anymore. I want to die.

I keep repeating over and over, "Shelly's not dead? She can't be dead!"

"What are you talking about Charles? Shelly will be coming here soon." Mandy reassures me my wife is safe and sound back in Ireland.

I wallow in my agony in the wooden tub for as long as Mandy will add an occasional bucket of hot water. She keeps water running over the top of the tub, so the slimy greenish yellow bubbles coming from my nose and mouth will float over the top and out onto the ground. Finally, after she is confident I am going to live to see another day, she brings me some clean clothes and a towel. She lays them in a neat stack upstream of the crud and goes back into the house to attend to her chores.

Mandy enters the kitchen, to find Bertha, Lila and Rose sitting quietly at the table pouring over a wrinkled piece of paper and an envelope. Mandy knows something is terribly wrong. She looks to Rose for an explanation.

"Charles' wife back in Ireland is dead. The baby died, too." Rose comes right out with the bad news. She hands Mandy the letter.

"Shelly's not dead. She can't be dead!" Mandy prays it's a mistake. She drops the letter and falls to her knees sobbing. Soon, she is a slobbering glob, lying on the floor moaning.

Bertha goes back around to the bath house to check on me. She uses a big wooden hammer to knock out the plug and drain the tub. Bertha decides to cover me with horse blankets and let me sleep it off right there in the bath house.

Before going to join Rose in the bedroom, Mandy makes sure all the liquor is hidden away from her bereaved brother.

The next morning, "Charles is gone!"

"He must have rode off on one of them chestnut geldings." Frank announces that half of the team that is broke to pull the carriage is gone, along with a saddle and a bridle.

"Well, you just saddle-up and go look for him." Mandy barks and order at Frank.

"No! Frank is not known well enough in these parts to go out alone, yet." Bertha expresses concern for her big man's safety. "Mandy, you and Rose go with him and he should be alright. Hitch the other Chestnut to the 'one horse' wagon."

"I'll hitch him up right now Ma'am." Frank is ready to go to town.

Mandy and Rose do not even think about disobeying Bertha. They change into their 'going to town' clothes and put their hair up under matching sun bonnets. Rose takes the reins of the one-horse buggy and Mandy takes a seat close beside her on the spring mounted wooden seat.

Frank's denim overalls with red striped gallowses that cross in the back and button onto the front bib are washed and ironed every day by Bertha and they have become his trade-mark. The big man takes his place on the back of the buggy looking rearward with his shiny black boots dangling near the ground. Rose snaps the reigns and yells at the little chestnut gelding causing him to rare up before he pulls the carriage away from the house. The trio kicks up a little cloud of dust as they hurry off toward town.

Soon after they go behind a little hill; just out of Bertha's sight, Rose stops the carriage and orders Frank to join them up on the front seat. He quickly obeys and climbs over Rose to squeeze in between the two ladies.

"Frank you and me need to get together for a roll in the hay sometime." Rose turns and looks Frank directly in the eye to let him know that she is not joking.

Frank gives his programmed response. "Yes'um. We'll do that for sure."

"Rose you bitch! You are nothing but a conniving whore." Mandy is devastated and deeply hurt.

"Well, I enjoy snuggling up to your pretty little titties every night, Mandy, but every now and again, I need a man – a big man."

"How would you like to be back out there selling yourself to anyone and everyone? I saved you from a life of hell and starvation, and you are not going to fuck Frank and then come back to my bed, ever."

"Alright! Alright! I was just kidding." Rose manages a slight smile and gives Frank a quick, "we'll talk about it later", look.

Frank is caught in the middle of a domestic cat-fight and he doesn't like it. Mandy senses his discomfort and reaches over and grabs the reins away from Rose. She pulls hard and yells, "Whoa"!

After the rig stops, she tells Frank it is alright for him to go back to his seat on the rear of the carriage.

"Yes'um," he mumbles as he climbs over Rose and moves to the back. Sexy Rose is aroused by his manly scent as his body passes close to her face, but she maintains her composure because Mandy is watching her every move.

As the noon hour approaches, instinct tells Mandy to look for her grieving brother down near the Sailing Ships in the James River Harbor. Her instincts are correct; they find his weary horse tied to a rail outside the "Oar House" bar in the rundown waterfront district. When the two proper ladies and their big slave enter the dark saloon it gets real quiet.

The bar tender gives us a quick look and yells, "Git the big nigger outta here."

"I'll go back outside and mind the horses – Mr. Charles' horse looks like he needs some water, anyway." Frank is not offended; in fact he has never known anything else.

He leaves without making eye contact with anyone.

Mandy can hear her brother's drunken voice coming out of the darkness over in corner of the damp, moldy room.

I am completely oblivious of the bar girl that is sitting on my knee with her arm around my neck. I am deeply engaged in conversation with a salty, well seasoned sailor who is just as drunk as I am. We are trying to decide the best way for me to get back to Ireland and visit the graves of my dear departed wife and child.

"Well, when you get sober, you just go down to the wharf and see Captain Bloom about signing-on with the Cumberland. He is hiring crew right now, and they are loading cargo for their return to Ireland. Be sure and sober-up first, Bloom don't drink and he don't hire drunks." My inebriated friend is slurring his words.

"Yeah. I'll get sober tomorrow for sure, and I'll go down there and see that sorry son-of-a-bitch, Bloom. He tried to get me hung for mutiny and murder, but I'm not holding a grudge." My words are slurring as well. My bloodshot eyes are moist and my nose is red and dripping. I have been repeating myself over and over for hours, but my inebriated friend remains very attentive and very sympathetic.

Rose glares at the bar girl and gives her a rude shove on her shoulder. "Get off him!"

"Who are you pushing, bitch!" The working girl yells.

With that, Rose rips into the girl. She drags her off my knee by the hair of her head and flings her onto the floor. The drunken bar-girl doesn't fight back; she just crawls toward the safety of the bar - cursing under her breath as she goes.

Mandy is impressed with her girlfriend's undiplomatic way of handling the situation.

"Time to go home now, Charles!" Mandy's tone is such that I decide to just get up and leave without putting up an argument. I am too drunk to sit up on the front seat, so Frank lays me out crossways on the back of the buggy.

Mandy and Rose head the rig for home – mission accomplished. Frank rides my horse, staying close behind the carriage. A lot of heads turn for a second look, as our ensemble passes though the cobbled streets of Richmond, and out into the lush, green countryside.

Our big put-together family has a meeting in the kitchen and we decide to get down to the business of running our giant plantation.

No one in our group has the appetite for buying the slaves necessary to plant, cultivate and harvest large crops, so we plan to rent out as much of the land as possible. We have gobs of fertile land that is cleared and ready for crops. We have hundreds of acres cleared for planting. Our share of the harvest will create a nice income and it will make us legit.

Bertha has formulated a master plan:

Charles will be the foreman and oversee all operations.

Lila will be the "1st Lady of the house" and the house boss.

Bertha will continue to play the part of Lila's personal servant.

Frank is charged with looking after the animals, the farm tools, the two barns and the many out-buildings.

Mandy and Rose will do housework, and run errands.

Lila and Bertha go about the business of buying new furniture for the house.

Everyone is engaged in work and enjoying getting things done, except me. I remain in deep depression over the death of my wife and child. Mandy and Rose have to drag me out of bed and keep all the liquor hid. I will not do anything without constant bitching and rib-jabbing from Mandy and Rose.

We receive an invitation to visit Colonel Jones and his family. The Colonel owns a huge plantation. Colonel Jones offers to have his workers bring-in some of the crops that have been standing in the fields all summer and divide the proceeds with us.

"There is a lot of corn out in the fields that has become much too mature for human consumption, but it will make great feed for the animals this winter." The Colonel allows.

The Colonel changes the subject. "Mr. McKenna, as I'm sure you know, over twenty years ago, the British came up from Chesapeake Bay through Bladensburg and burned Washington and the Presidential Palace. The White House has long since been rebuilt, but there are a few rooms that until this day have no furniture. My wife and I are having the Thomas Jefferson furniture, you so generously donated, reupholstered and refurbished. Mrs.

Jones and I intend to present the historic furniture to President Van Buren in hopes that it will help him finish furnishing the big house and you will be recognized as a co-contributor, my dear sir."

"Historic?" I have forgotten about donating the furniture.

"Yes, the furniture was designed by and originally owned by President Thomas Jefferson. Some of the pieces he actually crafted, himself. Jefferson was a man of many talents."

"Well there is no need to recognize me, Colonel. I'm just a poor Irish immigrant." I just don't even feel like an American yet. I still think of myself as Irish.

"You are not poor, Mr. McKenna. We are all immigrants in this wonderful new land."

"Well it's pretty hard for me to be cheerful, Colonel, my wife, over in Ireland, has just died in childbirth and my baby died too. As soon as I can, I am planning on going back to Ireland to visit their graves. I want to pay my respects and make sure my loved ones have been properly buried."

Colonel Jones is a little confused and concerned by the possibility of Charles having two wives simultaneously. But, since the two women are oceans apart, he decides to let it drop - for now.

I go down to the waterfront everyday and apply for work; trying to sign on as a crewmember to get me back home to Ireland. I have been drinking and looking for work; not a good combination.

My only experience is as a dish washer and cook's helper (except for that brief stent as pseudo Captain of the Cumberland). No one is interested in hiring me, partly because I was accused, albeit falsely, of murdering Captain Merritt and replacing him as Captain of the Cumberland. I was cleared of all charges in a court of law, but that doesn't seem to matter. I have been black listed by Captain Bloom.

It seems my career as an ocean going sailor has been nipped-in-the-bud, so there is no way to get back to Ireland. My depression grows deeper. The whiskey isn't helping, but I can't tolerate being sober.

Thankfully, Colonel Jones extends an invitation to take us to Washington to meet with President Martin Van Buren. The President has invited us to come spend the night in the White House. It's a gesture of thanks for the donation of the Thomas Jefferson furniture.

Mandy and Rose are excited. Bertha thinks it might be a chance to improve our station in the community.

Lila never gets excited about anything.

Frank is concerned about getting the animals fed and cared for while we are gone.

I manage to sober up some. Mandy helps me get all decked out in my summer linen suit with a Panama hat. I think I look the part of a prosperous Southern gentleman.

I am almost sober and just a little hung over, as we board the colonel's carriage.

Lila, Mandy, and Rose are all eloquently dressed as prosperous Southern ladies. They are wearing large hats with silk ribbon ties under the chin. Lila's baby bump is immediately obvious. Bertha's stiffly starched and pressed gray cotton dress is appropriate for her role as Lila's personal attendant. Frank is looking distinguished in a dark brown wool shirt and trousers with polished ankle length boots and wool socks. He is a fine looking man servant.

Our well dressed ensemble is loaded carefully into the large coach. We settle-in for a long, open air and bumpy ride to Washington, We will be overnight guest of the President of the United States and given a tour of the White House.

There are four matched black horses pulling our eloquent carriage. The horses manage to proceed at an easy gallop until about ten miles from home; then the road becomes rutted and the team must conform to a walk.

Colonel Jones and his entourage are waiting for us under a large oak tree near a country crossroads. The Colonel and Mrs. Jones offer a formal wave as they fall in behind us. The two carriages are very similar, except the Colonels' carriage is pulled by four matched white steeds and it is trimmed lavishly with decorative silver ornaments. The two carriages' create a formidable formation. It is evident we are on a mission of some importance.

It is a long and dusty trip. After a stop for a pick nick lunch, to colonel takes the lead. It is now our time to eat his dust for a few hours. We have colorful silk scarves for covering our faces.

The sun is sinking and the shadows are long as we roll onto White House grounds. The Colonel's wife is a little miffed when it becomes apparent that President Van Buren is not waiting at the North Portico of the White House to meet us. Instead, the President's eldest son, Abraham Van Buren, and his young wife, Angelica Singleton Van Buren, are waiting just inside the doorway of the North Portico. They come out smiling to meet our coaches. They are gracious and quickly offer thanks for the donation of Jefferson furniture.

President Van Buren is a widower. His wife died with tuberculosis several years prior and he has never remarried. Angelica, his daughter-in-law, and the beautiful young wife of his eldest son, Abraham, is the acting 'First Lady' of the White House.

Colonel Jones introduces us while Bertha and Frank go about their duties; pretending to be slaves.

Mandy and Rose both curtsey when introduced to Abraham – they mistakenly think he is President Van Buren.

I am impressed with Abraham, but I can't take my eyes off Angelica; she is beautiful.

Lila is pleasantly shy and ladylike.

Presidential whiskey comforts me in my room while the other look around the rose garden. I show up for dinner completely wasted.

Angelica invited her aunt, Dolly Madison, to join for dinner... Dolly requested that I be seated next to her.

"Mr. McKenna, I understand you are still grieving for your first wife." she begins. Dolly is famous for being forward and a little blunt.

"Yes Ma'am. I left her in Ireland and she died giving birth to my son."

"Who is caring for your son?" Dolly asks.

"He died too, Ma'am." Just saying the words make me tremble.

"Well, why don't you just tell me all about it? Talking is sometimes helps relieve the grief."

"Shelly was the most beautiful girl in the county and we were planning a life in America together, and now she is gone." I opened up and talked to Dolly for over an hour. I tell her about the day we made love by the river and how she stood by me when I was awaiting the hangman's noose.

"Tell me about your wedding." Dolly is a good listener.

"Shelly insisted on wearing her tattered cotton dress. It was the same dress she had on the day we first made love - we were on a blanket down by the river. She had on that dress and she was barefoot, happy, and just a little bit tipsy."

Dolly is surprised to learn that I know so little about the actual cause of death of my wife and child.

"We have agents in Ireland and I'll have Jimmy get you all of the details. If you know more about what happened, maybe you can deal with it better."

"Jimmy who?" I ask.

"James Madison, my husband. He is a former president." Molly chuckles at my ignorance.

"Thank you, Ma'am. I would appreciate that. I need to know if they were properly buried and their graves properly marked."

"Please call me Dolly." Mrs. Madison moves in close and she speaks sweetly.

"OK, Dolly. You call me Charles." I say softly and I punctuate it with a hiccup.

"One more question, my dear boy. What about your pretty wife, Lila? How does she fit into all this?" Dolly's is a bit confused and naturally curious.

"Lila is a very nice person and she is carrying my child, but we're just not in love Ma'am."

I open my mouth to say more, but wise lady Dolly puts her finger on my lips and whispers, "Hush darlin'! Let's go see what the others are doing."

President Van Buren makes a 'thank you for coming' toast at the beginning of the meal and then says very little. Later, while he is picking over his blackberry cobbler desert, he rises and says, "Will you please excuse me; I must attend to some important business."

"He's going to bed." Dolly giggles into my drunken ear.

Abraham and Angelica escort Lila; one on each side of her. Mandy and Rose are holding hands, and the Colonel and Mrs. Jones are third in line. Dolly and I bring up the rear arm-in-arm as the formal tour of the White House begins.

The next morning I awake with a vague memory of having had wild sex with Miss Dolly. It seems she had maneuvered me into a small servants' bedroom in the basement of the White House. I vaguely remember parts of what happened, but the rest is lost in my intoxication and the blissfulness of the moment. I have a vision of her locking the door. In the yellow light of a flickering lantern; she slowly removed all her clothes to expose a mature and very attractive, slim and curvaceous body. She was intent on easing my pain and sorrow and I was powerless to stop her.

I am just a naïve drunk, but I am smart enough to know that a sexual encounter with a powerful man's wife can put your life in danger, grave danger, so I discuss my predicament with Mandy and Rose. They just laugh and tell me it was just a dream.

"That could not have happened, Charles. You were right with us the entire time." Rose assures me. Mandy agrees. It was just a dream.

During breakfast I attempt to approach Dolly. She is pleasant, but she avoids making eye contact with me. I instinctively know that I must show discretion, and I must respect her position.

Five weeks later, God answers my prayers!

A messenger from Colonel Jones' plantation arrives at our house. The old graying black man is riding bareback on a big red mule. He states he has a message to deliver to "Mr. Charles":

"Ms. Angelica Van Buren and Ms. Dolly Madison request the company of Mr. Charles McKenna at the home of Colonel Jones - Right away!" He trumpets.

His mission accomplished, some of the air seems to leak out of the messenger. He slides off the mule and slumps toward the ground a bit, then turns and leaves for home, walking with a slight limp. He is leading the big red mule and he is talking to the mule like they are special friends.

Quickly, I saddle up my favorite stallion and gallop off toward Colonel Jones' plantation. I sit down with wise and attractive Dolly Madison and her young, beautiful niece Angelica Van Buren.

"Our agents in Ireland have discovered that your dear wife, Shelly, is indeed alive and well, and your baby boy is alive and well, also." Angelica comes right out with it.

I am stunned beyond belief - bewildered and confused. I seem to be out of my body and I can hear myself moaning and whimpering. I can see myself rocking back and forth in my chair with my hands tightly clasped together between my knees.

"Thank God - Thank God in heaven", I keep saying over and over.

The two ladies sit quietly with tears in their eyes. They wait until I start to regain my composure.

"We don't know for sure who wrote the death letter, but we think it was her Uncle Tom O'Malley. Shelly got a similar letter saying you were also dead – lost at sea." Molly was talking fast.

"I got a letter saying Shelly and the baby had died, and she got a letter saying I was lost at sea. That was no coincidence; someone was up to something!" I am trying to get these incredible occurrences straight in my head.

I was still trying to put things together when Dolly comes out with last piece of the puzzle and it is not good news!

"Shelly is now married to her uncle; that Thomas O'Malley man." Molly has distain in her voice.

"Married to her Uncle Tom? Good Goddamn! How could that be?"

I apologize for my language, but the two genteel ladies expected worse.

"Shelly knows now, that Mr. O'Malley has lied to her about your passing. She knows you are alive and she wants to come to you. We have a plan!" Dolly announces.

I lean forward and listen carefully.

"Our agents will sneak Shelly and the baby out of Ireland and onto an American war ship. They will bring her right to Virginia." Angelica is excited and waiting anxiously for me to put my stamp of approval on the bold plan.

"Hell yes! Let's do it. But, put the safety of Shelly and the baby ahead of everything." I am excited.

"Yes, of course!" Angelica assures me.

"Anything else?" Dolly asks.

"Like what?" I retort.

"What about this Tom O'Malley? He is easily the most despicable creature on the face of the earth." Dolly clearly wants revenge.

"We should send him straight to hell?" I can feel my eyes narrow and my teeth clinch.

"I'll let you talk to James about that. I know he has people in place to do that kind of thing." Dolly is pleased with my direct call for action.

Former President, James Madison, listens to me compassionately, but he regretfully denies my request to exact revenge on Tom O'Malley.

"It is simply not a matter of State," he apologizes, and he wishes me well as I am leaving.

Three short weeks later, Dolly reports with a big smile on her face.

"Mr. Thomas O'Malley was found dead in his barnyard, apparently trampled to death by his big bull, Rufus."

Chapter 8

* *

Shelly Comes to Virginia

"Low means a girl?"

Charles and Shelly Together Again

When the courier reaches Richmond, he finds us busily engaged in the running of the Big Spring Plantation. The sealed message is from Dolly Mason, so I go looking for his little sister – I need a little help with the reading.

"Shelly and the baby are at the Navy Base in Norfolk." There is joy in Mandy's voice.

"Are they coming?" I am jumping around like a five year old.

"No. She is still too weak to travel – we should go to her."

"Damn right we will. We will leave first thing in the morning."

When we reach the U.S. Navy Hospital, Mandy and I are appalled at Shelly's condition. She is 'skin and bones'. She is pale and weak and no longer looks like her young and vivacious self. In fact, Shelly is weathered and drawn and she is just too sick to care.

The nurse arrives with the baby and the room begins to brighten. He is a big handsome boy and his bright blue eyes are darting from side to side, checking out everything in the room. Mandy grabs her nephew from the nurse and carries him to see his father for the very first time. My knees go weak and I must be helped to a chair. I sit with his little guy looking up into my eyes and smiling at his father for the first time. The room is flooded with a tidal wave of emotion. Everyone, except Shelly, has tears of joy flowing unashamedly.

I was told four months ago that Shelly and the baby both died during a difficult child birth in Ireland and now I am actually holding my son in my arms; it is surreal, and fear it is just a dream and could all disappear in an instant. I am holding the little guy too tight and my nine month old boy begins to cry.

"My gracious he has a big voice." The nurse gently takes the baby. I put my face in my hands and offer a prayer of thanks to almighty God.

Earlier, during the long ride up to Norfolk, Mandy and I discussed our big problem; how are we going to explain the strange family arrangement to Shelly?

"Shelly is not going to like the fact that you have a pregnant wife waiting at home." Mandy chides.

"Well, we can tell her that I did not agree to marry Lila until after I got the letter from Tom O'Malley saying that she had died." I know that Mandy does not like to lie.

"That means your baby by Lila will be born four months premature." Mandy smirks.

"It could also mean that I am not the father of Lila's baby and she doesn't know when Uncle Tom posted that letter and we can tell her it got here really fast from Ireland… and, I really don't think Lila's baby belongs to me anyway." I have already given it some thought.

"Well, you can think what you want, but I am not going to deny my nephew." Mandy likes having little ones around.

"Bertha thinks Lila's baby is a girl." I grin at my feisty little sister.

"Why?"

"Because, Lila is carrying the baby really low."

"Does that mean it is a girl?" I ask.

"Most of the time, Bertha told me."

"Well, Bertha doesn't know everything. She also said you would never see Shelly again and here she is." Mandy remembers Bertha's morbid vision.

"Yes but, she was right about Shelly marrying her Uncle Tom! How in the hell did she know that was going to happen?" I wince at the thought of my true-love with another man.

"First we must explain to Shelly why wealthy and intelligent black Bertha must pose as a slave when she actually owns the 'Big Spring Plantation' and that she is the source of income for all our family members. We shouldn't say anything about Frank unless she asks; then we will simply tell her the truth."

"What is the truth?"

"Bertha had you buy him at the slave market, because she wanted a man – a big man."

"We will just tell her it is part of the culture," I add assuredly.

"It is complicated, but Shelly is smart and she will quickly sort things out for herself." Mandy concludes.

The first order of business after they return to the plantation is to explain to Shelly that Lila is only his pretend wife. They pretend to be husband and wife to make the plantation family look like a regular family for the benefit of the neighbors.

Shelly sees right away that Lila is pregnant, but she is not yet ready to ask us for an explanation.

Mandy and Rose take turns caring for the baby and Shelly begins to recovery. We sleep together from the beginning, but it is three weeks before she turns to me and gently places my hand on her breast. Soon it is like old times again, except better. It is better because Shelly is my true love and I adore my baby boy.

Plantation owner, black Bertha, doesn't like Shelly being there, because they now have to explain to the neighbors why Charles has two wives; one with a young baby and the other with a baby on the way.

Lila doesn't like having Shelly in the house, because she wants her unborn child to have a father in her life, and she is sure Shelly will never be willing to share. We are fond of each other and we are good friends, but we have never been in love. Lila was raised in a 'free love' community in the Caribbean Islands and she does not understand the strict religious mores' of the Irish. There is no way that Shelly can be expected to understand Lila's easy approach to relationships.

Rose keeps telling Mandy that the house is a time bomb and they are headed for a catastrophic explosion.

The next morning both of my wives show up in the kitchen and they are alone having a hot cup of tea together. It is their first opportunity to become acquainted.

"When is your baby due?" Shelly is genuinely concerned for Lila's welfare.

"Very soon now." Lila answers pleasantly.

"When is your baby due?" Lila puts the question back to Shelly.

"What! Why do you think I am pregnant?" Shelly stands and leans toward Lila waiting for an answer.

"I'm sorry. I shouldn't have said anything." Lila is embarrassed. She rises and leaves the kitchen.

Shelly is shocked at the suggestion that she might be carrying a child. She needs to talk to a girl, so she goes to Mandy's room and knocks on the door.

"Come in!" It's Rose's voice coming through the closed door.

Shelly is taken aback to see Rose and Mandy sleeping in the same bed, but she ignores it and asks the big question.

"Do I look pregnant to you?"

Rose declines to answer the question; she turns toward Mandy. Mandy sits up in the bed to take a look at Shelly standing there with her gown hiked up above her waist.

"Oh, my God, how did that happen?" Mandy blurts out.

With that Shelly collapses into an overstuffed chair.

"What am I going to do? How can I tell Charles I am carrying my uncle's child?"

"Just tell Charles it is his baby." Rose believes in taking the easy way out.

"If I am showing already, this baby could be born in about five months. It is not Charles' baby and I am not going to lie to him."

"We need to talk to Bertha." Mandy assures Shelly.

"Why?" Shelly is puzzled.

"Bertha is a Voodoo Priestess and she has had medical training and she is clairvoyant."

"Claire who?" Shelly asks.

"Bertha can see into the future. She told Charles and me months ago that you would marry your Uncle Tom and that you would never come to America." Mandy explains.

"Well, she was half right. After I got the letter that Charles was lost at sea, I married Tom for the sake of the baby. If I am pregnant this baby belongs to that lying bastard, Tom O'Malley. I am so glad he is dead!" Shelly is sobbing and a little ashamed of what she has just said.

After breakfast Frank goes to the barn to tend the horses; the ladies gather in the kitchen for some girl talk concerning Shelly's unwanted pregnancy. Soon after the conversation begins Lila begins to feel uneasy and out of place. She excuses herself and leaves the room.

"Bertha can you give me an abortion?" Shelly is desperate. The urgency in her voice gathers everyone's attention.

"Come over here, baby and let Bertha look at you better – slip out of that pretty gown."

Bertha looks closely at Shelly's vein lined breast and she probes gently on her puffy tummy. Finally she reluctantly shakes her head and answers, "no".

"It is too late for an abortion, child. It would just be too risky – you should have this child, it will be a blessing to you." Bertha tries to put a good light on a bad situation.

Bertha thinks Shelly should not tell Charles anything until he notices her getting bigger and starts to ask questions. "When he asks a question tell him the truth, but do not tell him any more than necessary."

Rose, on the other hand, advises Shelly to simply lie about everything for the sake of the child.

But, Mandy and Shelly agree that they should not lie to Charles. Instead they will wait for the right time to let him know what has happened and hope he can handle the bad news.

Lila hears everything from just outside the room and she decides that if they do lie to Charles she will tell him the whole truth, but for now she will remain silent. She fears for the safety of her unborn child and for herself. She has learned to fear Rose…

All the women are in Lila's room when her baby is born. The baby is a healthy little girl with a mop of long black hair. She obviously has her mother's complexion and she is beautiful. Bertha had taken over, as usual, and she delivered the baby without a hitch. Mandy and Rose have never seen a baby delivered. Mandy was amazed, but Rose was sickened. Shelly had been Bertha's number one helper and she was much too busy to think about what was happening until after the baby and mother were cleaned up and lying together under the warm covers of the big bed and looking lovingly into each other's eyes.

Lila names her baby Charlsie and Shelly doesn't like it one bit, so she decides to ask Lila the big question.

"Is my husband the father of this baby?"

"Yes, the baby girl belongs to Charles. Don't worry it will not cause a problem." Lila is tired and happy.

Shelly backs against the wall. She is amazed by Lila's frank admission.

Mandy has fully accepted her brother's illegitimate child, and for that matter, she is totally sympathetic of his girlfriend.

"Believe me Shelly, Charles 'did not know' Lila until after he got the letter from Tom O'Malley saying that you and your baby were dead." Mandy carefully recites the big lie that she and Rose have agreed to tell; even though the time line would make the baby very premature. Little Charlsie is obviously a full term infant.

Shelly is almost certain her husband had an affair with Lila before he got the letter. A letter declaring she and the baby had died and were buried together in Ireland.

"Did not know Lila? Do you mean 'he did not know her' in a biblical sense?" Shelly asks.

"Yes! That's exactly what I mean." Mandy's tone is a little crisp.

Shelly has always had the respect and the friendship of the women around her, but every female acquaintance she has in America seems to wish she would just go away. Her husband, her only friend, has obviously been unfaithful to her and he is lying about it, and she is lying to him about the child she is carrying, because the truth is too painful for her to reveal.

She married her Uncle Tom when she got a letter saying I was lost at sea.

Shelly mostly stays in her room, and when she is alone she cries, and repeats over and over, "What a mess! What a terrible mess! It is not my fault, Uncle Tom lied to me and I only married him for the sake of my baby."

Frank delivers Shelly's breakfast to her room and Shelly wants to talk.

"Frank how long have you known Lila?" she asks.

"She was here at the plantation when they brought me here from the slave market."

"You were a slave?"

"I'm still a slave, Ma'm. I have been a slave all my life. I was born a slave. My Momma was a slave."

"Are you and Bertha married?"

"Probably so, Ma'm. Yes – maybe, for sure." Obviously Frank doesn't know.

"Does Bertha own you, as well?"

"No Ma'm Negro's ain't supposed to own slaves. Mr. Charles is my master." Frank says proudly.

"Is Charles the father of Lila's child?" Shelly finally gets to the point.

"Yes Ma'm he is the father of that pretty baby girl for sure, and he sho is proud."

Shelly starts to cry. Frank leaves the room wondering what he had said wrong.

Frank returns to the kitchen where everyone is gathered, a usual. "I think Miss Shelly is thinking about jumping in the river. She is crying something awful." He announces.

"What's wrong?" I spring to my feet.

"She's mighty upset over Miss Lila having your baby, Mr. Charles, sur." Frank has never been more serious or confused.

"Well, she's got bigger problems than that." Rose's tone is hateful.

"Shut up Rose!" Mandy and Bertha yell in unison because they think Rose is going to tell Charles that his wife is pregnant with another man's child.

"What problems?" I am towering over Rose and demanding an answer.

Rose glares at Mandy and ducks under me and storms out of the room without saying anything.

"This place has been a mess every since Shelly got here." Bertha sighs.

"Dolly Madison will be here tomorrow; maybe she can help us get back the normal." Mandy loves Dolly – everyone loves Dolly.

It is true, everyone loves Dolly Madison. She is the reigning Queen of the Washington elite, even though her husband is no longer President. Dolly is smart, unpretentious and genuinely concerned about other people. She has a special knack for helping people who have desperate problems and she does it all from the goodness of her heart. She has never met Shelly, but she has been very friendly with me. She knows all about our life together in Ireland. After Dolly found out that Shelly's Uncle Tom lied to her and convinced her that I was lost at sea, she 'took care' of Uncle Tom and brought Shelly to America on a US Navy warship.

Dolly met me, and the whole family, when we came to Washington to tour the White House at President Van Buren's request. That's when she heard about Shelly for the first time.

Now, Shelly has locked herself behind her bedroom door. She is depressed and she will not answer Dolly's knock.

"She will open up when Charles come in from the fields." Mandy allows.

While they are waiting, Dolly is escorted to the formal dining room for tea.

"Let's go to the kitchen, this room is a little chilly." Dolly makes the request in her usual down-to-earth manner. She arrived in her riding clothes and when she sits, she props her muddy, leather, over the calf boots up onto the chair next to her. Mandy and Rose start to explain Shelly's problem to Dolly, but Dolly wants to talk to Bertha and Lila.

"Tell Lila to bring in her baby girl, I would love to see her."

The bronze Bahamian Princess comes into the kitchen cuddling her baby. The black Voodoo Priestess is right behind her.

"Bertha, I understand you are a Voodoo Priestess, how did you happen to become a slave?" Dolly gently takes the baby.

"I came into some money, so I gave Charles and Mandy some money and I just pretend to be their slave. With Charles as our white Master, we were able to purchase this big plantation. You know, Miss Dolly, Negro's are not allowed to be land owners in Virginia." Bertha risks everything by telling Dolly the truth.

"I met Mandy and Charles on the ship coming over from Ireland and fell in love with the sweet children at once." Bertha adds.

"What about Lila?" Dolly nods toward the Bahamian beauty.

"Charles met her when we stopped at her island in the Bahamas' to take on some fresh water. They liked each other right away and they made love the first day they met and now they have a beautiful baby girl."

"Naturally, Shelly would have trouble with Charles having an outside child, but Lila and Charles are not married. Are they?" Dolly looks at Lila, but Lila just lowers her eyes.

Bertha answers the question. "No. They are not married. We just told the neighbors they were married to make our family look legitimate."

"Well, no wonder poor Shelly is upset." Dolly offers.

"It gets worse, Miss Dolly." Lila finally speaks.

"Worse? How could it be worse?" Dolly raises her voice and the baby cries.

"Yes Ma'm. Shelly is four months pregnant with her Uncle Tom's baby." Lila just blurts it out.

"What! Tom O'Malley is a lousy, no good, son-of-a-bitch!" Dolly leaps to her feet obviously infuriated. She is still holding the baby and the wee-one begins to scream. Lila quickly takes her baby. Dolly has apparently lost her senses.

Bertha is quick to tell Dolly she should not curse the dead. "Tom O'Malley's spirit could come back and haunt you." Bertha is not the least afraid of the living, but she has a deathly respect for spirits.

"Yes, you are right Bertha. I should not curse the dead – but, I'm not worried about his spirit, because he is burning in hell for the awful things he did to Charles and Shelly - and now this. We should get her an abortion."

"Bertha has already checked her condition and she thinks it is too late for an abortion." Lila interjects.

Dolly looks at Bertha and Bertha shakes her head in agreement with Lila's comment.

I hear the ruckus and enter the room to greet my friend, Dolly. I am shocked when Dolly begins to cry.

"Charles we've got to talk, your so called friend, Tom O'Malley, was the most devious and wicked man I have ever encountered in my time on this earth." Dolly is a master at getting to the point.

"O'Malley is dead now, and the world is a better place, but he has inflicted pain and suffering on you and your family that is going to last for years and you will have to work to keep your family together."

"So if he is dead – what's the problem?" I am confused.

"This is going to hurt you deeply and if I didn't care for you so much, I would just go home and forget about it."

"Is Shelly sick?" I am horrified.

"Not exactly Charles, she is pregnant and the baby belongs to O'Malley."

I can/t speak, but my head starting to spin and my heart is pounding. There is a long confused silence.

"Tom O'Malley is her uncle; the child could be an idiot!" Finally, I spit out the words.

"Well, we have discovered that Shelly was never really a blood relative to Tom O'Malley. She had known for a long time that brother was not her natural father. Her mother was pregnant when he met him."

"What??" It takes a while for that to soak in.

"What about an abortion?" My head is spinning and my heart is pounding.

"It's too late for an abortion. It would put Shelly's life in danger. She has a good chance of having a healthy baby, but if you and Shelly are to have a happy life together, you must both accept this child and love it like you own. If you can't do that, your life will surely be miserable."

I am stupefied and unable to respond. Dolly softly blows her nose and wipes her eyes. She is clutching a linen handkerchief with a frilly edge.

"Does Shelly know all this?" I finally ask.

"Yes, and she is devastated. She is concerned about the pain this will bring, and how it will affect your future.."

My sister and I have risen from poor impoverished orphans to wealthy plantation owners in just a few short years. I am now reunited with my true love and we have a healthy baby boy; now this.

Mandy is happy and comfortable with her life, but I am not happy, nor am I content. I enjoy the financial comfort and security of the "family", but I do not feel at home with the flat and rolling topography of Eastern Virginia; I miss the rugged, hilly terrain of Ireland. I feel that slavery is an "abomination to mankind" and through circumstances beyond my control I have become a slave owner. Now, my wife is carrying another man's child. She was deceived; emotionally and physically raped by someone she admired and trusted.

During the ensuing two years, Shelly and I are miserable. It is uncanny how much our second child looks like Tom O'Malley. I am determined to accept the boy for Shelly's sake, but every day on the plantation is another day of deep discontent.

I want to take Shelly and the two boys west to the mountains. I start to discuss it with Bertha and Mandy.

"It will be hard to run the plantation without you, baby," Bertha insist. "Why don't we just build you and Shelly your own house right here on the plantation? That might make things easier for you."

"We would really like to move west and make our own way. If I had a horse and wagon, I'm sure I could find work around Roanoke." I am trying not to beg.

Eventually, I approach Colonel Jones' nephew. He is living with his uncle on the big plantation next door.

"Mr. Stewart, we are looking for a foreman to run Big Spring Plantation. How would you like the Job?" I insist he come over for a visit and meet the entire family.

Joseph Stewart is a tall, well educated gentleman. He is not the least interested in being a plantation foreman... Until he meets Lila and her baby daughter. Beautiful Lila lets him know she is available. Her big brown eyes say it all. Joe takes the job.

My next order of business is to make Frank a free man. I thought it would be difficult, but I am surprised when the biggest objection comes from Frank.

"Mr. Charles, I don't know how to be free. Why don't you just forget the legal stuff and leave me be your slave."

"You have Bertha, Frank. She is the smartest person I know. She will help you make the adjustment."

"Maybe I could go with you and Ms Shelly. You're going to need lots of help." Frank is pleading.

"Bertha is not going to let you go anywhere, and besides, she can't run the plantation without you."

"Does Mr. Stewart like Negros? He might be a mean boss man."

"Mr. Stewart is a fine man. I have talked to Bertha and she will be watching how the two of you get along. I know you will never complain, so Bertha will be watching."

"I don't like it. I wish you would stay."

"Frank, you are a smart, healthy man. You aren't going to have any trouble being free. Just be nice to Bertha and remember you are a married man."

"I will need a last name. Is it alright if I be Frank McKenna?"

"Yes.' I didn't see that coming.

I am truly going to miss my best friend.

Bertha gives Shelly and me what we need to make the long trip to Roanoke.

Mandy is devastated with events and she refuses to come out of her room with Rose.

I am very grateful to Bertha. She has provided us with a sturdy covered wagon and a team of big horses. We have enough cash to carry us for a few months and some gold in a strongbox. We are set for the trip to Roanoke and beyond.

Bertha and Frank are both hoping I will change my mind. "If things don't work out, you will always have a home here at the Big Spring Plantation." Bertha's eyes are moist and there is pain in her voice.

Tears are streaming down Frank's cheeks. He cannot speak.

Chapter 9

West to the Mountains

It isn't until we are out of sight and smell of the plantation, that I take my first full breath in months - a refreshing breath of relief.

We have been greeted by a cool morning breeze. The fiery orange ball rising across the rolling pasture sends a warming welcome. Morning mist is hovering on the horizon. Dawn's early light has cast a red glow on Shelly's beautiful white skin. Her long auburn hair is glistening in the sunlight. Sparkling curly locks have fallen across her slender shoulders, lightly caressing her bosom.

My beautiful wife is cradling her new baby. Our firstborn son, Will, is right behind us. Little Will is in the bed of the wagon cuddling his new puppy.

God has given me back my family, and because of them, I have taken an oath to never drink another drop of whiskey.

Colonel Jones presented us with two guard dogs just one week before we left the plantation. The Colonel gave us the big dog along with her six week old puppy. Will has laid claim to the puppy.

The puppy's mother is a large Russian Bear Hound and she likes jogging along beside our wagon. Her name is Boomer. Colonel Jones imported Boomer from Bulgaria. Bodacious Boomer is a big boned, long legged animal with a shaggy white coat. She has a huge head and a long floppy wet tongue. She weighs in at a whopping 115 pounds. The fun loving, magnificent bitch would prefer to be closer to her puppy, but she is happy running free; occasionally leaving the wagon for short sprints into the brush to check out small game and birds.

Our two giant Belgium draught horses are straining forward and pushing hard on the leather and chain harnesses. We have a big, beefy wagon and it is loaded to the hilt with stuff. The matched team of behemoth equine struggles to maintain a steady pace. There are two saddle horses stumbling along behind the wagon, champing at their tethers.

The going is slow. The big wagon squeaks, and it wobbles from side to side along the rutted dirt road. Shelly and I are full of anticipation; looking to start a new and exciting life. Life at the plantation had become much too complicated and much too stressful. Bertha didn't say a word, but I know she was glad to see us go, even though she was near tears when we left. Thanks to her generosity, and gifts from our neighbors, we are well equipped and well funded. We have all the necessities for a new home in the unknown.

The first day we make less than twenty miles and stop early. We come upon a small trading post, built to accommodate travelers. Shelly and the boys take a room inside the tavern. I intend to sleep in the wagon with the big dog, Boomer, by my side.

A young cowboy helps me take the gear off the horses. We brush them down a bit and give them water and grain. All four of our horses will be free to walk around and pick the short grass inside the big round corral until morning.

My supper of pork and pinto beans arrives from the kitchen right on time.

Boomer and her puppy are already dozing on a horse blanket beside the bun

Around midnight I am awoken by a huge ruckus out in the corral. The Belgium's are thundering around inside the rail fence. The saddle horses are running and bucking and staying close to the bigger horses.

The corral is a pit of swarming activity. I can hear wolves yapping and barking. The horses are whinnying and snorting. Suddenly, Boomer jumps across the tailgate, and out of the wagon bed. She races toward the corral and bounds across the rail fence. She flies into the midst of the frenzied wolves. It is easy to see Boomers' large white shape in the moonlight. The wolves are big and they are hungry, but Boomer is bigger and he is programmed to kill.

The tavern owner is yelling and screaming. He is trying to protect his yearling colt. Wolves have the little horse by his head and the tail and they are trying to get him on the ground.

Boomer races to the center of the fray and attacks the alpha male. She grabs the big warrior by his throat, and with a vicious shake of her massive head, Boomer breaks the lead wolf's neck.

Boomer slings the lifeless body aside and goes for her next victim, but the fight is over. Suddenly, all the wily predators scamper out of the corral. They scatter for a safe distance, before regrouping on a moonlit ridge. The hungry pack stands quietly for a while; looking back at us. They are dejected and they are mourning their dead sire – he was leader of their pack. One by one they disappear into the darkness.

The tavern owner checks to see if we are alright. "That big dog of yours saved my colt. Where can I get a hound like that?"

"Is your little horse alright?" I change the subject.

"Yeah, they had him by his snout, so his lip is ripped up some and one ear is bleeding, but he will be just fine."

"I saw two of those crazed critters chewing on the colt's hind quarters – they were determined to get him down."

"I'll check him over good in the morning, but he looks ok right now."

I lower the tailgate and give Boomer a short whistle. She jumps into the wagon and goes directly to her puppy.

It is a while before I sleep.

The next day we make good time —the road is getting better. Things come to a halt when we reach a fast moving stream. It is time for caution. I decide to saddle a horses and ride out into the water to test the current and gauge the depth.

It quickly becomes apparent that it is too risky to cross the stream. A grassy knoll nearby is cool and inviting. We set up camp, under a clump of poplar trees. We are on high ground and it is pleasantly comfortable. Shelly gathers fallen tree branches and builds a little fire to make coffee while I tend to the horses. Will is playing in the wagon with his puppy, and Boomer is resting on his blanket beside the fire. It is time to enjoy the end of a wonderful day — we gather our little family around the campfire.

The sun is about to dip below the horizon. Our bellies are full and a pleasing drowsiness has engulfed us; suddenly I am aware of strangers walking into our camp from three different directions.

"How you folks doin'?" A big red headed man with a tangled, bushy beard, stained with tobacco juice comes toward me. He is grinning and spitting.

I jump to my feet! All three intruders draw their weapons.

Boomer doesn't hesitate or interrogate; she leaps from her blanket and charges the big red head.

The intruders are startled by the unexpected attack by the big dog. All the bad guys turn tail and run. Big red is yelling and cussing - he is trying to free his right arm from Boomer's mouth.

Later that night, Shelly and the two boys are in the wagon asleep and Boomer and I are sleeping on the ground near the fire.

Swish! Thud! I hear strange sounds and Boomer has an arrow stuck in her chest. "She's dead." I hear myself saying – then nothing.

The next afternoon, I awake with Shelly holding a damp cloth to my bloody forehead. I try to get to my feet - I can't move. The next time I awake it is dark and quiet, and my head is throbbing. I can hear Shelly sobbing behind me and I call for her. My clothes are soiled and I ask her to get me some clean clothes. The dawn is breaking by the time she gets me cleaned; my clothes have all been stolen.

I pass out again in a fit of dizziness.

Later, Shelly is trying to get some chicken soup down my throat.

"What happened?" I ask.

"They took everything." She is sobbing.

"Did they take the wagon?"

"Yes."

"Is our money gone?"

"Yes."

"Is Will alright?"

"Yes, and Boy is alright too." I forgot to ask about Boy.

"How about you, did they hurt you?"

She cannot answer. She sobs and blubbers something I can't understand.

Two days later, I am strong enough to dig a shallow grave and lay Boomer to rest.

The river current has subsided, so I carry Will across the stream on my shoulders and go back for Shelly and Boy. We continue our journey on foot.

Our spirit broken; we are beat up and dejected.

As we plod along, looking for berries and fruit near the roadside, I smell smoke. Shelly smells it, too. It smells like a campfire with food on the spit. We are weak, hungry, unarmed and vulnerable. Shelly decides to crawl ahead and check it out. She returns without seeing anyone; just a smoldering fire.

We are looking toward the smoke when a voice behind us says, "You folks must have tangled with the Rattlesnake Gang." It's Curtis Rivers.

Curtis takes us in and saves our lives. He gets us into the little village of Roanoke. It was a three day walk to the little timber town. I rode Curt's horse most of the way, while he walked and helped Shelly carry the baby.

Roanoke has a good doctor. He properly cleans my wounds and puts me on the road to recovery.

Our 'Good Samaritan' is a handsome half breed. His mother is Irish and his dad a Cherokee chief. It is a good mix – Curtis is tall and slim with shoulder length straight black hair and a dark complexion. He has chiseled features and his mother's violet blue eyes. He was raised an Indian by his father, 'Big Rivers'. Curtis makes a good living hunting game. He works for the timber company and provides fresh meat to the timber crew. He hunts at night with a rifle, but he employs his bow-and-arrow and Bowie knife whenever he can. Curtis brings the fresh carcasses into the timber company's work camp around noon each day, and he stays to help with the butchering.

The company depends on the crafty woodsman to provide meat to the lumberjacks.

Finally, after I am beginning to feel fit, Curtis asks me to work his 'still'.

"Making liquor is hard work and I don't really like the job," Curtis explains.

I agree. It is hard work, but I need a job. I start gathering and crushing over-ripe apples to start the fermentation process. I start a big batch of slop working for a run of apple brandy. Curtiss has yeast and sugar in his shack and he makes sure I add the right amount to the vat at the proper time. Stirring the smelly goop with a big paddle takes up most of my day, but I am thinking about the Rattlesnake Gang.

"Curtis you talk like you know those Rattlesnake assholes."

"Yeah. I know all four of them…one of them is my cousin".

"Only three came to my camp."

"Yeah. Chester likes to stay home and drink and play with the squaws – he stays in camp a lot. Chester is the best shot of the bunch. He says he has killed forty men, but you can probably cut that in half."

"What about your cousin? Is he an Indian?"

"No. Buck is a red headed, white, son-of-a-bitch. Our mother's were sisters."

"Do you know how to get to Rattlesnake Hollow?"

"Sure, I have been up there a bunch of times. They live in an old trapper's cabin and they usually have five or six squaws up there doing all the work. The gang has a moonshine still out by the creek and they grow a vegetable garden, so they need squaws to do the work."

"Do they pay the women?"

"Sometimes, but mostly they work for food, liquor and sex. Chester takes care of the young ones, but the old squaws like to take on the donkeys."

There is a long pause while I digest that comment.

"Are you joking?" I finally say.

"No, they were all kicked out of their tribes for fucking donkeys."

I am curious. I want to hear more about the act of having sex with a donkey, but I decide to stay on track – I am leading up to something big.

"What happened to the old trapper?"

"They went up there and killed him. He was a good ole guy, too. He put a bullet in Buck's shoulder and cut his ugly face wide open with a butcher knife."

"I didn't see any scars on your brother's face when he came after me."

"That's why he grew that dirty red beard. He's covering up his mistake."

"How far away is Rattlesnake Hollow?"

"Too far - if you go up there, they will kill you for sure. Just forget about your wagon and money, my good friend."

"I am sure my wagon and my horses are up there somewhere. There is a lot of gold it that wagon. If you help me get it back, I'll pay you well."

Curtis explains to me that because of Cherokee folklore he cannot kill his cousin because his grandmother's spirit would torment him forever.

"Do you believe that bull?" I think he is kidding.

"Yes, I can't help you kill him." Curtis is serious.

I beg him to just go see if my wagon is up there. He finally agrees. The following morning he leaves on a pinto pony without a saddle and doesn't return until an hour after night fall.

Curtis found the wagon, but he is resigned to the fact that I am going to get myself killed.

"I have a plan for you. I want you to practice with my cross-bow until you can hit a gnat's ass at 100 yards. You might just come out of there alive with your stuff."

"What's the plan?"

"It's a plan to keep you alive. The old trapper built that cabin right on the edge of a cliff. There is a spring nearby. The water from the spring goes underground for a ways and then comes out of the rock at the edge of the cliff. Every morning, everybody in the house is hung over. They come staggering out the back door of the cabin, one at a time, and go over to the edge to take a piss. You can hide behind the wood shed and pick them off one at a time, then push the bodies into the crevasse. The next one that comes out of the house will not know what is going on. If you shoot good, you might get them all without a fight."

"Just pick them off one at a time?"

Curtis nods his head.

"What about the squaws?"

"You will have to kill them too – they are all mean as hell; they will cut off your dick and balls and then give you a pistol so you can shoot yourself." I cover my crotch with both hands.

"Damn. I never thought about having to kill a woman." The thought gives me chills.

"If you don't kill the women, they will kill you for sure." Curtis knows his people.

"I don't like it, but I guess I can do it." I still can't move my hands from my crotch.

I start practicing with the cross bow. My first practice is a good one, but I work with the bow for several days. I practice reloading the arrow over and over, and after a while, I am fast and I am deadly accurate.

"Should I wait for a full moon?" I ask Curtis.

"No, ride up to the mouth of the hollow in the daylight. Leave early, so Shelly can bring your horse back and then you walk up the hollow alone, after dark. Stop before you go through the gap, they may have a lookout there. Cross thru the gap as soon as you see the first hint of sunlight in the next morning's sky. Slip into the camp and get yourself set up by the woodshed in the back of the cabin." Curtis draws me a map.

"What about their dogs?" I ask.

"I didn't see no dogs. The squaws like to eat dog and they have probably already eaten your puppy. The place has a herd of wild donkeys. The squaws feed the donkeys just to keep them around. Donkeys get nervous when a stranger or a wolf pack of something comes on the place. Those little jackasses can bay loud enough to wake the dead, but they relax some when the sun comes up."

"The gang feeds a big flock of guinea hens. Guinea's make a hell of a racket when anything comes around, but they will be roosting in the trees and they will stay pretty quiet if you get in there just at daylight. If you try to sneak in there in the dark the Guinea's will make a lot of noise and someone will come outside to see what's happening." Curtis is clever, but superstitious.

I follow the plan to the letter and I am all set up behind the wood shed, but nothing has happened and it is mid morning. No one has come out to pee over the cliff. I wait patiently and occasionally I peep through a crack in the corner of the woodshed. My cross bow cocked and ready. The place is eerily quiet and I am getting hungry. I am tired of waiting.

The Guinea's are running all around me and they are starting to cackle and squawk, but not at me. It appears they are milling around the corn bin waiting to be fed.

"Maybe the gang is out on a raid." I'm thinking. "No, the squaws would be here working and I can see all the horses in the pasture." I hear myself mumble.

I decide to take a chance and peep in through the window.

I can see Curtis' red-headed cousin laying on the floor.

"He is either dead or drunk." I'm mumbling again.

Then I see one of the one of them laying on top of a little Indian girl. Someone has blown the top of his head off! "That must be Chester." I'm talking out loud. The girl moves a little. That startles me; she is naked and covered with Chester's brains and blood.

I lay down the cross bow, cock my pistol, and move toward the front door. It is cracked open a bit, so I give it a kick and jump back. I listen, but I hear nothing. After a short count, I dive inside. They are all in there, but they are all dead, except for the girl. She hanging to life, but she has obviously lost a lot of blood.

"She's a goner." I'm talking louder now. She hears my voice and she groans, but she looks to be beyond help.

I decide to go outside and look for my chest of gold and hitch up my wagon. The chest and the harness for the horses are no-where to be found.

I am confused and dizzy and I need someone to help me sort things out, so I saddle up a riding horse and head back to town to get Curtis and let Shelly know I am alive and kicking.

Shelly is waiting for me at the mouth of Rattlesnake Hollow.

"Oh, thank God, you're not hurt!" She is shrieking.

I am surprised when my true love doesn't ask about the wagon or the gold; those things don't seem important to Shelly, but I want our stuff back.

I tell Curtis everything, and he is smiling the whole time I'm talking

"You're alive! No one ever came out of Rattlesnake Hollow alive before this. You are the bravest white man I know." Curtiss is not joking.

"Well, I didn't do nothing – they were already dead when I got in there. Looks like they got in a fight and killed each other."

"Yeah, but you didn't know they were dead. It takes a man with big balls to walk into a venomous pit like Rattlesnake Hollow."

"Let's go get the sheriff and then go up there after my stuff."

"Not this sheriff! You don't want that crooked bastard up there – he'll hang you for murder and then steal all your gold."

"What if the sheriff finds the bodies? What will he do then?"

"The sheriff doesn't have the guts to go near that place." Curtis thinks for a minute. "Let's go up there and get your wagon and then burn the cabin with the bodies inside."

Vultures are circling the cabin and green flies are swarming when we arrive. Curtis is being very cautious even though he knows they are all dead. The Guinea's are squawking and cackling and the donkeys are baying.

The first thing we do is water and feed the horses. I show Shelly where the corn bin is and she feeds the Guineas.

"If there is anything of value on this place, it will be in the root cellar." Curtis is walking as he talks. "I know where they keep the key."

No need for a key. The root cellar door is cracked open and we can see my chest just inside the door. The chest appears to be locked and there is a squaw's body in there right beside it. There is a heavy yellow mist hanging inside the damp underground cellar.

I hold my breath long enough to dash into the hell hole and carry out my chest. On the way out I spot the key laying beside the body of the squaw. I run back in and pick the key out of the dirt. I try not to look at her or breathe until I am back outside. All this time, Curtis is standing twenty feet away, bent over and laughing.

We eventually find everything – even our puppy. The puppy has grown and he looks like he has been fattened-up. I offer him water, but he just licks my hand.

Our happy group heads for home with the flames leaping from the wood shingled roof of our improvised crematorium. Two hours later, we are just a half mile from the safety of Roanoke and we have our stuff.

"I thought those scoundrels stunk real bad enough when they was alive, but they stunk a lot worse when they was dead." Curtis is still laughing.

Shelly and I are happy to have our money and wagon back, and I am happy I didn't have to kill anyone. We are happy, but we are not laughing.

Chapter 10

* *

Shelly and Curtis

With my help, Curtis' wood fired moonshine distillery has miraculously converted the big batch of fermented rotten apple slop into a clear and potent apple brandy. News travels fast, and the entire thirty gallons of the high proof, crystal clear liquid is quickly disbursed. It is eagerly consumed by the dedicated drunks in the village of Roanoke and beyond. I have made Curtis a large chunk of money and it is obvious to me that he expects me to start another batch right away. I hate the monotony and hard work of making liquor, and being around the stuff has weakened my resolve to never drink alcohol again. So, I give Curtis notice, and quit working the still after one batch.

I hire on as a mule-skinner's helper. Dragging huge logs out of the forest with a team of fourteen mules is more my idea of a real job. Everyone knows that mules are stubborn and plenty smart. Working with mules, you must be patient, but determined. I begin my workday before daylight every day. My first task is to pick the most able mules and hitch them in pairs of two to create a team of fourteen.

We have thirty three mules in our corral. Every beast has a name and a distinct personality. Most of our mules are a reddish brown color. The rest are black or a mix. Every animal picked for work on a given day know their place in the line-up. Most of them go straight to their position and wait for the harness. There is one red mule that knows exactly where to line up, but he refuses to move toward his place until I give him a little smack with the whip. He always balks until I slap him on the rump. Then he gives me a light nudge with his nose and moves directly to his spot in line. Another mischievous red mule always lines up facing backwards. He waits for me to turn him around, and then I must pat him on the head, or he will follow me until I do.

If mules could smile, I'm sure these two would be snickering at me every morning. Once in harness the mules work harmoniously as a team.

We are lucky to have a skillful mule skinner. He knows how to avoid the pitfalls. The mule skinner and I work in concert to bring the big logs quickly out of the woods and into the yard. When the big logs are being skidded along the ground there is always the potential for an unexpected happening. Mules get hurt and must be destroyed, and people often suffer injuries as well. My job is to jog along beside the team and look for trouble. I must stay sober, focused and alert; I don't want to get caught when a skidding log unexpectedly rolls sideways.

I work long hours. The pay is good and it is hard work. An important part of my job is to hook (and unhook) the chains to the logs and I am required to help pry the logs free when they get stuck in a ditch or up against a stump or rock. My tools are a razor sharp double bladed axe and several big pry-poles made from ash or hickory.

The timber company has built a mobile camp for the loggers - twenty shanties in a row along the creek with about eighty inhabitants. Shelly and I, and the two boys, occupy a make shift home. Our house is a wood frame structure covered with canvas. Everything is in one room. All the cooking is done outside. We keep our wagon and our horses behind the shanty. We have a milk cow to nourish our boys. Shelly milks the cow and she has planted a vegetable garden. Company chickens are running wild everywhere and everyone feeds them with table scraps. The company encourages each family to help themselves to a chicken or two for dinner every Sunday. Will likes to gather the eggs for our breakfast – he has learned where some of the laying hens have hidden their nests.

Curtis shares the shanty next door with two older men. One of the old guys works as a butcher and the other is in charge of caring for the company pigs. The timber company has a large pig farm. Sometimes pigs get out and wander around the camp sniffing for food.

Curtis makes sure my family gets fresh cuts of meat several times a week.

We have a water barrel in the front of the house and it is kept filled with fresh water by a company operated water wagon. They bring cold water from a nearby spring fed stream every day.

I work in the daytime. Curtis hunts at night. He is home most afternoons, while I am working. He goes to bed in the early evening and slips out of the camp on his pinto pony after midnight to go hunting. The timber company pays my stealthy half-breed friend well for providing fresh meat. The loggers and their families are well fed.

I notice that Curtis has taken a liking to our youngest son, 'Boy'. Shelly wants to pick a name for him, but I like calling him Boy. He is a toddler now, and he is a developing a broad chest and a large head like Tom O'Malley. He is a fine looking youngster, but I can't bear to be around him. Shelly is well aware of my feelings and it is obvious that I am not his father.

"Why do you give all your attention to little Will and ignore Boy?" Shelly loves both her boys.

I don't answer her, and I don't look at her.

"Boy is getting bigger now. When he reaches for you, you just walk away. It hurts him, I can tell."

Shelly continues, "I married Uncle Tom when I thought you were dead, but I never intended to have Tom's child. I am so sorry, please forgive me." She is sobbing.

"Well, you don't have any reason to be sorry. You were lied to, and you were deceived. You did what you had to do to survive. I will be sure and pay more attention to Boy. It's not his fault either."

"I can't believe my Uncle Tom could be so mean. How could any human being be so evil? He lied to both of us; he even wrote you that I was dead and that little Will was dead, too. I saw him kill my Aunt Sally. He smothered her with a pillow when he thought I was asleep. I saw him do it, but I first thought it was a dream – a horrible nightmare." Shelly repeats this over and over each day.

"Well, he did it because he wanted you in his bed. Tom's dead and he is now paying for his sins. Let's try not to be tortured by his memory."

"Well, Boy isn't a memory and his mere presence seems to torture you." Shelly is looking at her feet and sniffling.

"I love you, and both our boys, more than life its self - nothing is going to change that." I'm sure this is the first time I have ever told Shelly I loved her and it brought a tear to my eye. I didn't want her to see me weeping.

"It would help if we gave him a name and stopped calling him 'Boy'".

"I agree. Let's name him after your father. What was your dad's first name?"

"I don't even remember my dad; he died when I was very young. I think we should name the baby Curt." Shelly looks me directly in the eye.

"Curt?" I'm shocked.

"Yes, Curtis saved all our lives and Boy just adores him!" Shelly is adamant.

"Why not just call him Curtis?"

"I like Curt better. It will be less confusing." It is settled; Boy finally has a real name. His name is now Curt.

Curtis is pleased that Boy has been named after him.

Curtis and Shelly sit out front by the creek and talk after lunch. When I come home from work, the three of us sit and talk. We watch the two little boys play in the dirt. Shelly cooks supper over an open fire. Around dusk we sit down as a family and eat. It is a happy time.

Curtis usually has had a snoot full of whiskey before he goes to bed. He turns in early and gets up a little after midnight to begin his nightly search for deer and small game.

It was several nights later, around one o'clock in the morning, I wake to discover Shelly is not in her bed. When I go outside to look for her, I hear a faint giggle. It is the same sweet laugh she did when we made love in the barn loft back in Ireland years ago. I treasure that memory, and it always arouses me.

Suddenly, I hear a horse galloping out of the camp, and then I see them ride through a moonlit clearing. They are riding bareback and Shelly is holding on tight behind

Curtis. They disappear into the shadows. I know my life has changed forever.

The blanket Shelly and I first made love on flew off the horse as they galloped away. I stand over the blanket and let my tears fall before I kick it into the scrub.

It is near dawn when Shelly finally returns to her bed. I lie quietly and pretend to sleep. In a short time, I can hear her rhythmic breathing. My darling deceitful Shelly is asleep.

I stay awake staring into the darkness until sunrise. I struggle out of my bunk and head down to the creek to try and sort things out. A lot of time passes, but I am paralyzed. The sun is getting hot. I am surprised to see Curtis coming down the path toward me.

"Are you going to work today? They have sent a boy to see if you are coming to work." Curtis is talking and walking toward me.

"Where did you and Shelly go last night?" I'm trying not to show my anger.

Curtis doesn't answer. He turns and starts back up the hill to the camp.

"I'm talking to you - you lousy half breed!" My anger explodes.

Curtis stops and comes back toward me for a few steps. He pauses and sits down on a log. In a second, I am standing over him. I demand an explanation.

"Your wife is unhappy – she just wanted to talk last night." He says calmly.

"Talk? You don't talk to my wife at midnight out in the woods ever again - you understand! Besides, you talk to her too damn much every day right here in the camp. Stay away from her!"

"I promise you, I will stay away from her, but you need to get closer to her my friend – Shelly feels you have drifted apart because of her baby. She is very lonesome. Shelly needs a friend. Go to work now, and think about what has happened. We will try to sort this out tonight after you come home from work."

Shelly is pretending to be asleep, so I take his advice and go to work. All three of us will have time to settle down and get our thoughts together before I come home.

"Yes, I do love Charles, but I have fallen in love with you too, Curtis. Is that possible?" Shelly is confused.

"Yes, it is possible, even natural. It is a common practice among the Cherokee people. Women and men often have more than one lover. It only works when everyone is in agreement – there is sometimes a little jealousy, but never any deceit. I don't think Charles will ever agree to share you with anyone. I think you and I should break it off for your sake and the sake of your two boys." Curtis hopes Shelly will disagree.

"I cannot stop loving you Curtis, as long as you are near me." Shelly reaches for his hand.

"Then I'll just go away, before someone gets hurt bad." Curtis pulls his hand back.

"I'll go with you." Shelly is truly desperate.

"No. He would come after you because of little Will. He doesn't care that much about you or Boy, but he would spend the rest of his life trying to find Will. He would become obsessed with killing me, and he might end up killing all of us."

"Boy's name is Curt, and you are right, Charles despises my baby boy."

Curtis just nods in agreement.

"I could never leave little Will behind - I could never abandon my firstborn child. Not even for true love."

There wasn't much talk when I came home that night. I was much too angry and shocked to think straight and they were afraid they would set me off.

We all start drinking, but after one swig of white lightning Curtis gets up and leaves. Shelly and I get pretty drunk. The boys are asleep and we are all alone. We try to make love, but I am unable – nothing is rising in me, except my resentment.

I don't sleep much that night. Shelly gets up and goes outside around 2am. I follow her. She goes to the toilet. I check the shadows for Curtis. He is not there. Shelly staggers back to her bed she falls asleep quickly.

Early the next morning I leave for work with a hangover and a lot on my mind.

Waking up in a hospital bed is frightening, and I have no idea how I got here. The bandage on my head is too tight and it is hurting my skull. I can see that my left leg is elevated and in a splint.

Eventually, I remember I was trying to turn around the red mule that always lined up backwards, but I don't remember anything after that.

The mule skinner had found me unconscious. He thought I had been kicked in the leg by a mule and then stomped on the head while I was on the ground. He said I had been kicked a lot and he was sure I was dead when he first saw me. The mule skinner put me in a wagon and brought me to the hospital.

I had been unconscious for eight days.

The two older guys that live with Curtis come to visit me in the hospital. Somehow, I am not surprised when they tell me that Shelly has left the lumber camp with Curtis. They didn't take little Will. They left the little guy with a lady in the logging camp. All the ladies in the camp have been taking turns caring for Will. He is crying for his mother day and night. I need to get well quickly and go to him.

"Did they take my wagon?" I don't ask about the gold. I'm sure I will never see it again.

"They filled your wagon with junk and took it with them. They took all your horses and the cow. Curtis' pinto pony followed along behind them, but it walked back into the camp the next morning. So, I guess it belongs to you."

"Why did they leave little Will? I know Shelly loves him." I am mostly talking to myself.

"Curtis kept telling your wife that you would come looking for them if they took Will away; she finally agreed to leave him, but she never stopped crying after that."

"Well, as soon as I can walk, I am going to go find them and cut that half-breed into little pieces and feed him to the hogs.

While my leg is healing I have a lot of time to think. I spend time consoling Will and trying to explain to the little guy why his mother left him. During that time, I prayed to God for the judgment to do the right thing. Eventually, I decide to try to forget about Shelly and concentrate on making a life for Will and me.

"Now that is the Christian thing to do." The old butcher man says. The pig-keeper nods his head in agreement.

Taking care of Will without a woman in the family is a big job, but everyone in the timber camp helps me look after my motherless child.

A young widow with two small children is constantly bringing me and Will food. She is very nice to Will and he sometimes calls her Mommy. She is a fine lady, but I am full of hate and resentment for all women.

After a few weeks of rest and healing, I am ready to head west. I find a saddle for the Pinto and we set out on foot. When Will gets tired I put him on the pony. I am completely broke, so we will be living off the land as we travel. I am hoping to make Abingdon, a village in the foothills of the Appalachian Mountains, in a week or so.

Living off the land is easier than before. Curtis taught me how to trap rabbits and squirrels and how to select berries and plants that are edible and tasty. Will likes to roast small game over an open fire. One evening I shot a huge turkey with the cross bow. Will and I cook up some choice turkey parts in a pot. Finding ginseng root and making a tasty hot tea is a treat for us. Little Will likes ginseng tea. He loves the wilderness and we have never spent so much time together. We are very close, but he sometimes cries for his mother.

Seven days on the road and we arrive in Abingdon. We are both well and hardy. Being alone in the wilderness has soothed me some. I have communed with God more than ever before in my life. I know, I must forgive Shelly and Curtis, and wipe the hate from my heart, before I can find happiness in my new life. It is hard for me not to hate them, but I am hoping time will help me forget and forgive.

Land is available for a hard working man to homestead in this western part of Virginia. My dream is to homestead a place in the hills that takes my spirit back to my birthplace in Ireland. I will work the land and build a home for Will and me.

Curtis knew of my dream to go west and he had told me many times, "Be sure you don't go too far and cross over into the 'Dark and Bloody Ground'. They call it Kentucky. The Cherokee only go in there to hunt, but they always come out before the night falls."

"My grandfather would never stay overnight in Kentucky – grandfather was taught by his Cherokee elders that the 'dark and bloody ground' is possessed with powerful spirits." Curtis was serious and I remember everything he said.

I look for a family to board with in Abingdon; a place where I can work for room and board.

I find a room for rent in the Baker home. There is an attractive young daughter in the house. Amanda helps look after Will while I am working. She is sixteen years old, and a bit of a tomboy. Little Will takes to her quickly. Miss Amanda Baker was born in Belfast, but she came to America with her parents when she was 2 years old.

"My father goes into Kentucky often to hunt and put meat on our table." Amanda stands very close to me when she talks. I like her.

Chapter 11

❋ ❋

Amanda

"The Cherokee say Kentucky is full of angry spirits. Many animals and Cherokee warriors have been killed in there." Mr. Baker is puffing his pipe.

"Has most of the game been killed off already?" I ask.

"Heck no! The place is swarming with elk and deer. You can get a four months supply of meat in just one day. I always hire a couple of Indians to go along and field-dress the deer and elk."

"I thought President Jackson drove all the Indians out of Virginia and across the Mississippi River to Oklahoma."

"The old bastard didn't get all of them." Obviously, Mr. Baker didn't care for Andrew Jackson.

Amanda's dad continues, "Just before you get to Kentucky, there is some beautiful and rugged country still available for homesteading. You should stop in Wise

County. It is due north of here and it is still in Virginia. It too, is a land of plenty, with an abundance of wild game; it is blessed with cool, fresh, fast moving trout streams. The streams are alive with fish. There are outcroppings of coal that can be harvested for heating your home and cooking. There are acres and acres of big timber. The mountains get bigger as you go north. Wise County is close to Kentucky, but far enough away, so you will not to be bothered by angry spirits."

The more he talks the more anxious I am to get started.

"It is just two days ride from right here. From Wise County you can cross through Pound Gap right into Kentucky and get back to camp before dark. Most of the white men, and all of the Indians, come out before it gets dark."

"Pound Gap?" I have never heard that name.

"Yes, Pound Gap is the easiest place from here to cross the Cumberland Mountain Ridge into Kentucky." Mr. Baker likes to talk and I am anxious to learn.

"Do you think I can I find land to homestead in Wise County?"

"Sure. Just go up there and stake it out. Then go into Gladeville and file your papers at the county court house.

"When would be a good time to leave here?" I definitely like what I am hearing.

"You could go next month. October is a good time to explore. The turning of the leaves in those mountains is something to behold. You can stake out your place and come back to my house for the winter. Then you can go back up there in early spring and build yourself a cabin, so you will have shelter before the winter snows start."

"Can I leave my son here with Amanda?"

"I don't think your boy would like that. Why don't you take Amanda and the boy with you? She has been up there before, and she can take care of your son. Amanda has even been hankering to have a child of her own. Her mother has been awful worried about her. Amanda has been looking for a man since she filled out and haired over."

"Does she have a man?" I can hear Amanda giggling in the next room.

"No, but her feelings for you are powerful strong." Mr. Baker's forwardness surprises me.

"I like her too, but she is too young to be of much help. Would you and your wife approve of her going off with me into those wild mountains?"

"Yes, I would approve, but you got to get married first."

I wasn't expecting that.

Mr. Baker senses my surprise.

After a short pause he continues, "You seem to be a level headed, fine young man and there ain't much for her to pick from around here. And anyway, if you try to homestead a place up there without a woman to help you, you are sure to get yourself hurt or killed. My girl can shoot – she can hunt – she can cook – she can split rails and chop wood. She don't know much about being married though, you'll have to teach her about that. I will have her mother talk to her and explain some things and you can do the rest. I'll tell her to do exactly what you say for her to do. She can be a little head-strong sometimes."

"Well, I just don't think any of that will be a problem, but she still seems pretty young to me."

"Amanda is good stock. Sure, she is young, but she is healthy and strong like a man. She is just the right age to provide you with the strong boys you will need to survive in the mountains. You will need a big family with lots of boys and girls. You've got to get the crops in, and get them put-up, to make it through the cold winters without starving."

"Amanda! Come in here." Mr. Baker sounds angry.

"Yes, Paw." She is pretty and she is smiling. She doesn't look at me.

I think this is the first time I have ever really looked at her as a woman. Maybe that is because she always dresses like a boy. Tonight she is wearing denim over-alls over a red plaid shirt with gallowses across her full bust. Her straight brown hair is short and glossy. Her big brown eyes sparkle and she has an almost dark complexion. Her teeth are straight and they are white. Amanda has a pretty face with fine bone structure and high cheek bones.

I start thinking about what she would look like naked and I feel a little unwanted twinge.

"Daughter, would you like to marry Charles and move up into Wise County?" I appreciate the old man proposing for me, but this is an awkward moment.

"Yes Paw, I sure would." She smiles bigger, but she still doesn't look my way.

I feel a bigger twinge. This one jerks my knees a bit.

The following Sunday, we get married in the Baptist church. Amanda's mother has never spoken a word to me. She sobs through the entire ceremony. I find out later, she doesn't want her daughter marrying a Methodist.

The little church is full of people and it is hot. All the windows are open and the doors on both ends are propped open, but there is not much air moving except the preacher is a little too windy. He finally winds it up and says, "You may kiss the bride."

We kiss. It is a short, but a sweet kiss.

Amanda is bubbly and happy. She is a beautiful bride and she looks all grown up in her mother's wedding dress. I'm surprised and delighted with what has happened to me. I had resigned myself forever to a lonely single life.

On our wedding night, I find out she is not shy about doing what comes naturally. I ask her, if her mother told her what she should do. Amanda laughs and shakes her head "no".

When she finally quits laughing, she says, "I saw it all in the barnyard. I saw them 'doing it' and I saw lots of babies being born and like Pa says; I can shoot, I can hunt, I can cook, I can split rails and chop wood, and now I know I can make my man happy."

"I love you Charles, I've loved you from the first time I saw you."

I know I am supposed to say something, but nothing comes out. Things are moving fast, and I still feel like I am married to Shelly. Needless to say, little Will is a somewhat confused, too.

Three days later, my new bride and I are ready to set-out for Wise County. The girl can ride a horse like an Indian brave. She has Will on the saddle in front of her and he is beginning to like his new mom. We are going on a mission to 'stake out' our new home.

Mr. Baker has loaned us two saddle horses, a pack mule and three big dogs to go along with us. The pack mule is loaded with our provisions.

"Daniel Boone always hiked into the wilderness with a big pack of dogs. A bunch of his dogs was killed by wolves in a big fight right here in Abingdon. The wolves were living up there in Wolf Cave." The old man points toward the mountain side."

"Boone's favorite trail into Kentucky was through Cumberland Gap. Cumberland Gap is west of here, but he did go north though Pound Gap a time or two. Daniel Boone wasn't afraid to stay in Kentucky for months on end. He settled up there after a while." Amanda's dad is excited, and he is talking too much.

We finally wave goodbye and ride away. I can see Amanda's mother standing in the doorway... still crying.

We plan to ride north all day and stop at dusk. I navigate by the sun, but I still wonder at times which fork to take when the trail splits.

It is a little after high noon and we are resting at a fork in the trail. Without a sound, two teenage boys come by on foot. Amanda whispers to me, "Cherokee".

"Kain tucky?" I ask the boys for directions with a one word question.

They laugh and point both ways. They are headed south in a hurry; I didn't like the way they looked at our horses. The boys came down the right fork, so we head up the left fork. I don't want to run into a big mess of Indians, if I could help it.

When the shadows begin to lengthen we set up camp by a tiny stream. Amanda has a flintlock pistol hanging in a holster across her chest and she slides it around under her arm pit when it gets in her way. There are lots of rabbits and squirrels running around our camp, so I set my rabbit trap.

Bang! Amanda kills a squirrel.

"Where did you hit it?" I am looking for the bullet hole before I skin it.

"I barked it. Don't worry about taking the bullet out. I just hit the tree bark right underneath the squirrel and the bark flew up and killed it – you don't mess up the meat that way.

"Damn. That's good shooting." Amanda is proud she has pleased me.

After little Will goes to sleep with his belly full of squirrel meat and rabbit stew, Amanda and I cuddle under the stars. We are enjoying the flickering fire. The horses and the mule are quiet, and the dogs are dozing in the shadows.

We make love as the moon crosses the brilliant starlit sky. Amanda is quite a handful when you get her going. It is easy to light her fire. She can't seem to get enough of my loving. It is the first time we have made love out of earshot of her parents.

"My little girl bride is quite a woman." I say to myself. I go to sleep warm and happy.

The next morning Amanda makes a big breakfast of bacon, eggs, biscuits and gravy. She knows how to function as a housewife and she can do it without a house - out in the woods. I was determined to live out my life grieving for Shelly, but today is a wonderful day.

After breakfast, we get going and cover a lot of ground. At dusk we set up camp along the banks of a trout stream and before I can get the horses taken care of Amanda has fish in the frying pan.

"Little Will caught our fish for dinner." Will is dancing around the fire flinging his arms in the air. Amanda has taught him how to fish. We enjoy our meal in the firelight.

It is quite dark when the dogs start barking. I hear a voice coming from the thicket.

"Hello! I come friendly. Can I warm by your fire?"

I motioned for Amanda to hide behind the mule. She takes her pistol from the holster and cocks it.

"Yes. Come on in. Keep your hands where I can see them." Are you alone?" He doesn't look like a bad man.

"Yes. I was fishing and I slipped on a slick rock and got soaking wet. Sure would like to dry up some by your fire?"

Amanda came out from behind the mule. She is putting her pistol away and greeting the stranger with a smile.

"My name is Dotson. Noah Dotson. Is this pistol-tottin' girl your daughter?" He returns her smile.

"No sir. This is my wife. She is older than she looks. We have a two year old boy, by my former wife. The boy is asleep." Mr. Dotson is a little concerned by Amanda's youth.

"Well, she sure has pretty brown hair." Amanda and Mr. Dotson exchange smiles again.

"Are you looking for elk? I can guide you to the herd."

"No. We are looking to homestead a place in Wise County and build a farm. We are planning on settling down."

Noah Dotson doesn't comment, instead he looks us over again. He looks around at our livestock and our belongings.

"What do you call this country?" I ask.

"You are in Wise County, Virginia. You are camped on Cranes Nest Creek, just a half mile from my place."

"Is there any land around here that hasn't been claimed?" I'm hoping for good news.

"Yes, there is some, most of what is left is pretty hilly, though."

"How far is it to Kentucky?" I am concerned about getting too close to the 'dark and bloody ground'.

"It's about twelve miles. You just take the Indian trail up through Pound Gap." Noah is amused at my concern.

"I am looking for a place with good water. Hills don't bother me, I love these hills. It reminds me of my home back in Ireland."

"Well there is some available land right near here on the river." Mr. Dotson says.

"On the river." I repeat and try to sound interested.

"Why don't you come spend the night with me and I'll show you around tomorrow?" He is very hospitable.

"That's very nice of you, but it is late, and we have had a long day. I think we will spend the night here." I am thinking of another night under the stars with my new bride. Amanda's eyes show her approval.

The next day we go find our new friend.

Noah takes me to a nice plot of land with over 900 feet along the creek. It has twenty acres that are level enough to farm, with a nice house place on a rise in the middle. Amanda stays behind to help Mrs. Dotson butcher a deer and prepare supper.

It is good bottom land, but I know it isn't for me.

"I like the high ground, Mr. Dotson. Do you know a place on a hill with water on it?" I am desperately hopeful.

"You know, there is a place just like that. It has already been homesteaded, but I think the people left it and moved back East. The law says they have to live on it, so it may be up for grabs again. Do you want to go take a look?" Noah Dotson is certainly a helpful man. I'm thinking he must feel the need for more neighbors.

It's an easy three mile jaunt for our horses. I am taken by how much I like the property. It is a rolling plateau perched on the top of a steep mountain. The climb up is challenging, but when you get up there, there is a big bubbling spring that feeds a sparkling crisp and fast moving steam. Two or three acres have already been cleared for farming and the foundation of a stone house has been laid and abandoned. There are several deer grazing on the property. We see elk tracks. I have found my home.

Mr. Dotson helps me find the corner stakes of the property before we return to his house on Cranes Nest Creek.

Mrs. Dotson and Amanda have prepared a nice supper for us and it is on the table five minutes after we get back. I sense that Amanda is a little miffed.

"What's wrong," I ask. "Did the old lady treat you bad?"

"No, she is very nice. From now on, I want to go with you when you are out in the wild. I am a good shot and you could get ambushed." Amanda is sincere.

"You can come along tomorrow. I am going to the courthouse in Gladeville to homestead the property." It sounds reasonable to me, but Amanda is pouting.

"Don't you think I should see the place first?" She says.

"Why?" I'm puzzled.

"Because! I am part of all this, too!" My young sweetie is pissed.

"Yes, you are part, but not this part."

She storms out of the room and I realize that we have just had our first quarrel. I don't like the feeling.

We make up later that night in the Dotson's squeaky bed. I don't know if the other people in the house heard us, but we made the dogs bark.

It is a long scenic ride to the county seat, so I decide to take Amanda by the homestead on the way to the courthouse and we will make a two day trip of it. Noah goes along to show us the way.

Amanda likes the property just fine. I show her where we will build the house; over by the spring. She is happy, so we don't stay long.

It is a winding ride, following the creek, through the narrow valley to Wise. I am glad we have a guide.

Soon after leaving our mountaintop we spot four men on horseback. They only have three horses, so two are riding double. They all stop and dismount when they see us coming.

"It's the Mullins boys. Let me do the talking." Noah says in a low voice.

"How you boys doing today?' Noah uses a friendly tone.

"Fair to midlin'. How 'bout you Mr. Dotson?" The oldest of the group spoke. He was showing respect.

"Been out working your still, boys?" It is obvious they are all drunk.

"Yes sir. We've been working it hard and running some good whiskey.

"What happen to Jack's horse?" Mr. Dotson changes the subject.

"We got hungry – had to eat Jack's little mare."

"Couldn't find you a deer?"

"I guess so, but Jack's horse was more handy and a lot more tasty." They all laugh, except Jack.

The Mullins brothers are talking to Noah, but they are all stealing glances at Amanda. The youngest brother, Billy Don, swaggers over to her horse. He reaches up and grabs her right arm and gives her a yank. Before I can react; Amanda draws her pistol with her left hand and fires – point blank. Billy Don's hat goes flying and his greasy long blond hair has a bloody part right down the middle of his surprised head. He thinks he is dead for a second. He isn't dead, but he isn't ready to try and stand up, either.

It happened so fast, I figured I would have to shoot somebody, but they are all just rolling on the ground laughing; holding their bellies and slapping their thighs.

Mr. Dotson motions for us to slowly ride away. "They're good boys, but awful bad to drink. Their daddy is a God fearing Baptist, and a good friend of mine. Jack's been a little quire, ever since he came down with the fever and that Billy Don is the meanest of the bunch." You can sense Mr. Dotson's disappointment with the Mullins boys.

Our homesteader's paperwork is filed at the courthouse without a problem. We are welcomed by everyone we meet. It seems Wise County is anxious for its population to grow.

We return to Abingdon to spend the winter. Our first child is born in the early summer of the following year. Amanda and our baby boy are well cared for in her parent's home in Abingdon. Mrs. Baker smiles an approval toward me for the first time while she is holding her new grandson.

Will is thrilled to have a little brother. "I'm going to teach him how to fish and ride a horse."

The trees are budding and the birds are chirping. I decide to go to Wise County alone, and start work on the log house. I know Amanda and the baby are in good hands.

Amanda is mortified by my plan to go alone. She asks her mother to care for the baby, so she can go with me. Mrs. Baker knows her grandson needs his 'mother's milk' and affection. Wisely, she refuses to keep her grandson away from his mother.

Mr. Baker advised against my plan to go alone. "It is too dangerous to work in the wilderness alone – you can get knocked-down by a timber or a big rock or even a horse and get all crippled-up. Then the wild hogs and wolves will finish you off." That brought back some bad memories from Ireland and made me change my mind about going up there alone.

Amanda and I agree to wait a month and then take the new baby and little Will with us.

The long trek over sea and land is at last over for me. I have found a home in my new land and I can finally settle down. Amanda is uncomplicated, but resourceful and talented. She is the soul-mate I never expected, but have needed badly. She loves life; when I thought my life was over, she came along and gave me a reason to live again.

It is hard work and we endure hardship, but with the help of our almighty God, we raise a big family on that beautiful isolated mountaintop in the hills of Southwest Virginia.

Charles McKenna was only 46 years old when he was killed during the Civil War. He rode with the 'home guard' during the historic Battle of Cranes Nest. He was defending his property when he was shot and mortally wounded by rebel marauders. Charles was carried home by his sons. He died in his house on his beloved mountaintop with a grieving Amanda and his children by his side.

In the years to come, many generations lived and died, on that bountiful Mountain.

Charles and Amanda still rest there today.

A Way Yonder
A Novel by Dick Blizzard

List of Characters:

Charles McKenna:	Young Irishman immigrates to America.
Mandy McKenna:	Sister who confesses to a murder she did not commit.
Shelly O'Malley:	Charles' true love.
Tom O'Malley:	Shelly's conniving uncle.
Captain Merritt:	Captain of the Cumberland.
Mr. Bloom:	1st Officer and Navigator of the Cumberland.
Mr. Games:	Young Naval Officer.
Bertha:	Wise Voodoo Priestess.
Lila:	Captain Merritt's beautiful daughter.
Rose:	Frightened prostitute adopted by the family.
Frank:	Bertha's big man.
Curtis:	Handsome half-breed.
Little Will:	Charles and Shelly's first born.
Boy:	Shelly's unwanted son.
Amanda Baker:	Charles' 2nd wife.

About the Author

Captain Dick Blizzard was a Delta Airlines pilot for thirty-three years. He retired as an international captain, flying the MD-11 from Portland, Oregon, to Asia. Dick started his flying career as a naval aviation cadet and served as naval aviator for seven years. He made over two hundred carrier landings and served with the Sixth Fleet in the Atlantic Ocean and the Mediterranean Sea.

Dick is licensed by the US Coast Guard to command ships up to one hundred tons. He cruised the West Coast of the United States from Alaska to Mexico with his wife (the admiral) for twenty-one years. Their fifty-three-foot twin-diesel yacht was docked in the San Juan Islands of Washington State.

Captain Dick was born and raised in an Appalachian coal-mining region of Eastern Kentucky and now lives with his dog, Nibbles, on the Alabama Gulf Coast. He attended Pikeville College, in Pikeville Kentucky and the University of Miami.

Captain Dick Blizzard now spends his time writing, speaking, and touring the country in his RV.